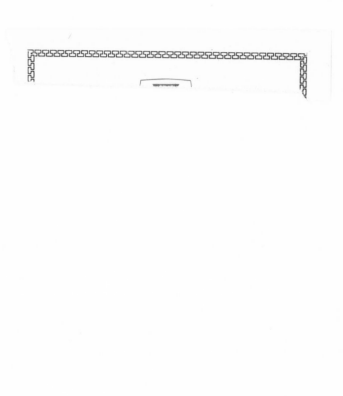

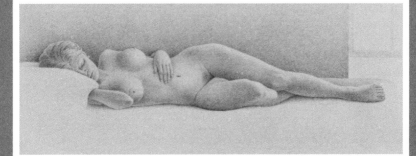

Edited by David Helwig & Maggie Helwig

COMING ATTRACTIONS

90

Acknowledgements: "all I ever wanted was the moon" by Sara McDonald first appeared in *New Quarterly.* "The Battle of Midway" by Steven Heighton was originally published in *Paragraph* and "A Protruding Nail" by Steven Heighton first appeared in *Writ.*

ISBN 0 88750 821 9 (hardcover)
ISBN 0 88750 822 7 (softcover)

Cover art by Christopher Pratt
Book design by Michael Macklem

Printed in Canada

PUBLISHED IN CANADA BY OBERON PRESS

Peter Stockland lives in Quebec, where he is a correspondent for the *Toronto Sun*. He has also worked as a reporter in BC, Alberta and Ontario. His fiction is sometimes bleak but always powerful, maintaining a degree of tension unusual in a new writer.

Sara McDonald was born in Saskatoon and now lives in Montreal. She works mainly in "postcard stories," with a fine comic touch, though "all I ever wanted was the moon" demonstrates that she can handle a more extended narrative equally well. And "jenny's iud is picking up signals from space" is surely one of the best titles in recent Canadian literature.

Steven Heighton of Kingston is turning out books at a frightening rate—he has published two collections of poetry so far, and his first book of short stories will appear soon. Heighton has lived in the Far East, and now edits *Quarry* magazine while working as a waiter in Kingston's only Japanese restaurant.

Both Heighton and Stockland have previously appeared in *Best Canadian Stories*.

As a final note, I would like to dedicate this anthology to the memory of Bronwen Wallace, my co-editor for *Coming Attractions 89*, who died of cancer last summer. She is greatly missed.

MAGGIE HELWIG

PETER STOCKLAND

Greetings from Papineauville

It is already Sunday evening. The middle of May. Still quite warm. And quiet. Peaceful.

Achille and Coco walk up Rue de L'Eglise. They climb the small hill from the river. Both of them hold fishing-rods in their left hands. In his right hand, Achille holds a grey cord with a large silver hook on it. The hook pierces the gills of three fish. The fish turn speckled brown bodies in slow revolutions.

The street divides around the patch of grass and the blue reflecting pond that is Parc St-Sauveur. Achille unhooks the largest fish. Coco hooks a finger through the gill. The fish trails him home, its tail skating above the dust.

Achille walks another block until he reaches Rue des Patriotes, the main street of Papineauville. Its west end leads to Ottawa. Its east end leads to Montreal. He turns back. In a single motion he waves goodnight to Coco and tosses his cigarette away. It glows behind him. Smoke floats from it after he is gone.

"Christ de merde," Jules says. "Maudite bande d'anglais sales chien de bâtard."

He hangs upside-down on a Jungle Gym in the playground of L'École Louis-Joseph Papineau. As he speaks his T-shirt descends like an upside down curtain over his face. Christiane waits until the red cotton covers his eyes, then slaps him on the bare stomach. Her fingers leave a red mark almost the colour of his shirt.

"Tais-toi," she says. "Arrêtes de blasphèmer. Tu me casses les oreilles, toi."

She slaps Jules again, catching cotton this time as he swings up to avoid her. He drops to the ground upright, grabbing her left hand at the wrist. He pulls her toward him and tries to

8

hold her and avoid being hit at the same time. He kisses her, laughing. She breaks free and stands outside the circle of the apparatus, laughing.

He sings:

Les maudits anglais tête-carré,
Baptême, baptême.
Les maudits anglais tête-carré,
Baptême, baptême
Les maudits anglais tête-carré,
Je souhaite pouvoir les tuer
Les maudits anglais shit de tête-carré.

He laughs as loudly as he's sung. His voice carries over the lawn and across Rue des Patriotes. A woman in white running-shoes has one hand on the door of Dépanneur Turgeon when she turns toward the sound. Christiane runs across the grass covering her ears. Jules follows her, his voice bounding ahead of them both.

Ghislaine slits the white fish belly and spreads the flaps. She hooks two fingers into the cavity. Bright burgundy guts trail the fingers back out. They soak into the copy of *Le Droit* she's spread across the table. The newspaper ink mixes with the blood on her finger, blackening the red. She cuts the head and tail off the fish, then carries them out to the back porch. In the last evening light, she drops them into the cat's bowl.

Achille calls from the hallway. He's going to the dépanneur to get some cigarettes for the morning.

Coco guts and washes his fish quickly and wraps the refuse neatly. He walks outside and stuffs the bundle in the garbage can, tamping the lid down to keep out the raccoons and cats. The metal grunts and grinds. Through the kitchen window, he hears the television coming from the living-room. He goes inside and sees his wife asleep again on the sofa. He gently pushes her lower jaw up to close her mouth. She rouses at his touch. She falls back to sleep.

Two men get out of the green Chrysler that has pulled up across Rue des Patriotes from a white frame building. The sign has been taken off the building, but the outline of the letters still identifies it as Garage Félix. One window has a crescent-moon hole in the lower right corner. Behind the glass a red-and-black sign says *À Vendre*.

The man in the navy suit who was driving the Chrysler stands in the middle of the street waiting for a blue Chev half-ton to pass. His companion, also wearing a navy suit, catches up to him. At the door of Garage Félix, the larger man stands back and lets his smaller companion enter first.

Ghislaine stretches the Saran Wrap tightly over the white plate on which the fish lies. Water turns soap to bubbles on her hands beneath the tap. Achille comes up the walk as she settles into a chair on the front gallery. When she raises the match to the tip of the cigarette he gives her, she can still smell river water, weed, fish blood, on her skin. He slumps in the chair beside her. The twin red tips of their cigarettes mark them. They talk quietly about having the fish for supper tomorrow night.

"Bourassa vendu," Jules says. "Christ de merde vendu."

He sits on the wall in front of L'Ecole Louis-Joseph Papineau, drumming the heels of his Converse high-tops against the concrete. Christiane sits beside him. The zipper of her quilted ski-jacket is done up to her chin.

"Arrête-moi-donc," she says. "Parles pas de politique. Je n'ai rien à faire avec la politique. C'est ben plate."

Jules' friend Roger stands with his back turned to them. He watches a man tie a spaniel to the post outside Garage Félix. A woman in a white sweater takes the man's arm and they enter together.

Roger drains a can of orange juice into his mouth. The aluminum clanks hitting the sidewalk. It's the sound the empty beer cans made hitting the wall behind the arena last winter when Roger got drunk before the game against Hawkesbury. The juice can grinds and snaps when he crushes it with his foot. He turns to Christiane.

"Indépendance," he says. "Québec libre."

He smiles at Jules. Light and cigarette smoke drift out of Garage Félix when a man in a red-and-black plaid jacket opens the door and steps inside.

Coco clicks a leash onto the silver loop of his dog's leather collar and tugs. The dog rises slowly, shakes so that leash and loop jingle like Noël bells. He snorts. Snuffles. Walks up to the corner beside his master in a bedroom-slipper shuffle. His head is bent at a sharp angle to the grass. His eyes blink sleepily.

The larger man in the navy suit is marking numbers in an itinerary book. The smaller man is trying to find someone who'll take charge of turning off the television when the premier arrives at Garage Félix for his speech. A tight circle is watching the set at the far end of the room. They butt cigarettes nervously into crushed styrofoam cups. The Quebec Liberal party has rented Garage Félix for the by-election. Four volunteers spent Saturday converting the abandoned shop into headquarters for their local candidate. Laying clean plywood on the floor. Setting up tables. Putting up an equal number of posters showing the candidate and the premier. Finding a place for the coffee urn. Buying styrofoam cups. But the Canadiens trail 3-1.

Steam rises from the spout of the coffee-pot and curls around Ghislaine's face. She pours milk into Achille's cup. Only half a teaspoon of sugar. His blood pressure. He taps her lightly on the bum when she puts his coffee down. The premier's face looks up at her. It lies flat on her kitchen table. A small image of a smiling man in glasses surrounded by typewritten words on the front page of *Le Droit*.

"Il sera ici ce soir, hein?" Achilles says. "Monsieur le premier ministre."

The page rattles when he turns it. His coffee slurps when he drinks it.

Coco sees the kids leaning against the low wall in front of the school. He waves, but they don't see him.

Looking down the block, he sees a knot of people standing outside Garage Félix. There's a car he doesn't recognize parked on the other side of the street. He goes into the dépanneur and buys milk for the morning. Cheese for his sandwiches. Cigarettes. Four Molsons to help him sleep.

"Qu'est-ce qui se passe là-bas?" Coco asks. "Pourquoi il y a du monde devant l'ancien garage?"

The woman behind the counter stops a finger in mid-air above the cash register.

"On a d'la grande visite," she says. "Le premier ministre. Monsieur Bourassa."

Coco sniffs. He shifts the brown grocery bag to the crook of his left arm. The woman's finger punches the keys.

"Bourassa," he says. "Innocent."

He holds out his right hand for his change.

Christiane watches Coco bend at the bicycle rack outside the dépanneur and untie the dog's leash. She sees him slowly straighten and start home. The little dog pads at his master's side as if he'd rather be sleeping on his front paws than walking on them.

She turns on Jules, on Roger. Tells them they're idiots. That they talk nonsense.

"Niaiseux," she says. "Vous avez des têtes à Papineau, vous autres. Indépendance. Québec libre. Les vraies têtes à Papineau."

"Ben oui," Jules says. "Ma grand-mère était une Papineau. Son nom de famille était Papineau. Je pense pas que c'est la même famille, mais quand même. Ouai, j'ai une tête de Papineau. C'est une bonne tête. Pas comme toi, Christiane Cauchon, grosse tête de cochon."

Roger laughs loudly at the pun. At Jules having the nerve to insult a girl. The two boys light cigarettes. The smoke Jules exhales clings in Christiane's hair. She waves a hand in front of her face to clear it, and coughs theatrically. It leaves his taste in her mouth.

Ghislaine puts the fish on a lower rack in the fridge and makes room for the milk. She sees an ad in *Le Droit* for fresh spinach on special at Provigo in Thurso. She says she'll get some tomorrow to go with the fresh fish. Achille says he can pick it up on his way home from the mill. He says put a note in his lunchkit, otherwise he'll forget. He slips an arm around her waist. Smacks his lips.

"Des bons épinards avec une bonne truite," Achille says. "Hein, ça serait bon, ma femme."

The small man in the navy suit stands beside the set sipping coffee. He says the premier will be inside in about five minutes—he's just outside meeting people and shaking hands. The large man in the navy suit looks between the smoke that hangs from the roof and the heads of the people sitting at the paper-covered tables. He signals his companion. Larry Robinson lets a shot go from the Bruins' blueline. 3-3.

Jules holds Christiane's right arm tightly as she pulls away. Her arm comes out of the ski jacket's black sleeve and he's left holding the empty quilted cotton. He tries to catch her by the left wrist, but she moves back too quickly and he tumbles clumsily from the wall. She warns him she'll leave if he goes with Roger. She's not laughing now.

"C'est pas drôle," she says.

Roger kicks the empty juice can. It skitters and clacks down the sidewalk. When it stops, it turns slowly once on its axis.

"Viens, ti-Papineau," he says. "On s'en va."

He wants to cross Rue des Patriotes to Garage Félix and yell something. He wants to get up close to Bourassa's face and holler something that will make the people near the premier give chase. He wants to run. Run like hell down the street. Jump over hedges in front yards. Duck 'round the corners of houses.

"On va lui donner un bon 'greeting' de Papineauville," Roger says. "Comme les Patriotes de quarante-sept."

Jules looks at Christiane. She is already half-turned away from him. He looks at Roger, then across Rue des Patriotes. The window light spilling from Garage Félix mixes with the harsh conical floods of two television cameras. In the shadows between the two lights, the premier's arm comes up, reaches out into the darkness for another hand to touch.

"Quarante-sept?" Jules says. "Trente-sept. C'était en trente-sept, les Patriotes."

His grandmother gave him a book once called *Les Patriotes de Trente-Sept*. He remembers reading how Papineau urged his rebels to rise for La Petite Nation—the name of Papineau's seigneurie, the name of his dream. He remembers reading how the English slaughtered Papineau's Patriotes in the bitter winter of 1837. How they hanged the others after the rebellion failed.

Roger waves his hand impatiently.

"Un détail," he says.

Christiane turns her back.

The large man in the navy suit reaches across the head of the man closest to the set and turns off the game.

"Les Canadiens vont gagner," he says with the hearty certainty of a man who works for a majority government.

Jules remembers his grandmother's finger pointing. It was the flesh of her hand, in the Sunday evening light, that made him realize for the first time how old she was. He was fishing with his father from a small bridge over Rivière de La Petite Nation. They'd all gone to Huberdeau to buy early summer corn, and stopped to fish on the way back.

His grandmother got out of the station-wagon and crossed the bridge just as a fish struck Jules' line. Kneeling to free the hook, he saw the hem of her pale grey and coral dress above her thick brown stockings. Turning, he saw the creases in the leather of her bitter-smelling black shoes. He was looking up, pinning the wet, flexing fish to the ground with one hand, when she pointed.

"Ça—ça c'est nous-autres," she said.

The fish flipped free and Jules had scrambled to grab its slick flesh. His grandmother was back in the station-wagon when he looked up again. She sat beside his mother in the rear seat, turning stiffly to look out the window once or twice.

He and his father teased her for a bit, asking her what she'd meant. Asking her what they were? Birds? Hydro poles? When she wouldn't answer, they stopped teasing. They were silent down all the long hills home. Fields and trees, sometimes water, streamed past.

Coco sets the empty beer bottles in the cupboard case on the back porch. He leaves the outside light on for Roger. He leaves it on, too, for his eldest son Michel. He leaves an upstairs hall light on for his wife. It frightens him when she tries to find her way upstairs to bed in the dark.

The small man, the large man, stand side-by-side under the cigarette smoke, smoking cigarettes of their own, glancing at their watches. Sweat trickles down one's short, dark neck. Sticks under the armpits of the other. They were supposed to be in St.-André Avelin at 7.30—two hours ago. One says at least they won't have to compete with the hockey game now. It'll be long over before they arrive. The other says unless there's overtime. They both nod. Les maudits playoffs. Always bad news for spring by-elections.

Jules' grandmother sat on the back stoop. Woodsmoke drifted toward her from a small fire his father had started to cook the corn. There was a large silver pot of water beside her. The pot had a hooped handle. The handle hung from a hook attached to an iron rod arched over the fire.

He was crossing the yard to put the fishing-rods and tackle in the shed when he heard her tearing open the corn. The backs of her pale hands were ridged, the texture of the tough green leaves she parted. She ran her fingers over the conical cob, cleaning away the white-yellow filaments stuck to the knuckle-shaped kernels. She sang softly, under her breath, a children's song about water.

She might have been singing to the corn cobs she pulled from the burlap sack. When she spoke, it was absently, as if to the light.

"La rivière," she said.

Jules stood in the drifting smoke. His eyes and throat stung with dryness.

"Grandmama?" he said.

She might have been dead the way she didn't answer.

She was dead when he understood what she meant. When he understood it was the water she'd pointed at from the bridge. In her eyes they were the river. All of it: water, fish, name: La Petite Nation: Papineau's greeting: Papineau's dream.

Coco bunches his pillow under his head. Lies on his left side. Then his right. Back and forth. Lies on his back. Gets up and pees the Molsons. From his bedroom window he can look down Rue de l'Eglise and see the unlit space that's the river.

Roger will go soon. Michel already lives in western Canada. Somewhere called Tsawassen. Everyone in Papineauville laughed, at first, trying to pronounce the name of the town where Coco's eldest boy lived. Tswassen. Now, Christmas cards arrive signed: Seasons Greetings/Joyeux Noël—Mike and Cynthia, Tania and Jason.

Roger looks across the street. The premier is going inside. He's making his way forward in the darkness through a small circle of supporters backlit in the doorway.

"Vas-y, Jules," Roger says. "On peut dire en anglais: 'Greetings from Papineauville, Mr. Bourassa.' Quand il se tournera, comme un sale chien anglais vendu, on peut y dire en pleine face: 'Va-chier maudit anglais vendu Bourassa les Patriotes de Papineauville t'haïssent.' Ça va être l'fun, eh, ti-Papineau?"

Christiane turns back.

"Je m'en vais," she says. "C'est pas drôle."

She squints at the crowd. Names some of the people. Asks Jules if he thinks they'll just let him insult the premier. If he thinks they'll just stand with their hands in their pockets while he runs away laughing.

She turns away. Takes a step. Another. The quilted pattern of her jacket will disappear if she takes a third. If Jules lets her go, the next time he sees her she won't see him. He calls to her to stop.

His ankle hurts from his tumble off the wall. He felt something grind inside when he fell. He doesn't know how fast he could run anyway. He takes two hobbling steps. Turns to Roger.

"Juste crie fort d'ici, Roger," he says. "Ça serait mieux."

Roger has the loudest lungs and strongest throat in Papineauville. When he came in the arena drunk last winter and cheered for Hawkesbury, people in the seats around him covered their ears as if a car horn were stuck. But Roger has already stepped off the curb. His left foot already rests on Rue des Patriotes.

Christiane takes another step. Turns to look over her shoulder.

"Vas imiter ton petit chum, Jules," she says.

He takes a step toward her. Looks again at Roger. A drift of woodsmoke comes from somewhere down the street.

The premier himself enters Garage Félix. Supporters mill, begin to applaud. He moves inside, slowly, in a cone of television lights, beaming.

Ghislaine writes the reminder on a yellow Post-it Note before she goes to bed: EPINARDS. OUBLIE PAS. She tucks it in the fold of the wax paper covering Achille's sandwich. She puts an apple in, and sets the lunchbox on the backporch shelf. The cat jumps off a green-cushioned chair and trots toward his bowl. When he sees Ghislaine is empty-handed, he stops and looks appalled at her treachery.

She turns out the lights, checks to make sure the back door is unlocked for Jules. He'll catch hell in the morning for staying out late on a school night. But she isn't going to lock him out.

Her nightdress is cool against her breasts. She shivers, sliding into bed. She curls against Achille. Achille rolls onto his back. Even asleep, he feels the safety of Ghislaine beside him. He lets his breath out slowly, like floating up for air.

Jethro was a Bodine

Allan is whistling "Stairway to Heaven" when he sees the hood of his car is raised. He does a shuffle step to avoid dropping the platter of steaks. He stops whistling and walks quickly around to the patio. Wendy's shoulders are pinched as if the gas barbecue is something nuclear that could split her genes.

"What are you afraid of?" Allan says. Spits of smoke spiral into his eyes as he forks the cold meat onto the hot rack. "It won't explode."

"Turn it down," Wendy says, twisting the burner dial. "Why did we buy this thing, anyway? I liked our charcoal one."

"What's he doing?" Allan says.

He pushes steaks around on the rack. Wendy looks around as if someone has jumped the back fence.

"Who?" she says. "Turn that down so the meat doesn't burn. What's who doing?"

Allan pokes the fork tines at her. Asks if she wants to do it herself.

"Jeff," he says, "He's doing it again."

"What?" Wendy says. She peeks around the corner and down the driveway, then looks at Allan. "He's not doing anything. I told him we had a problem with the heat-thing on the car. He's just checking it."

Allan turns the steaks. Wendy paints them bright brown with barbecue sauce. Allan drops the tongs and heads down the driveway.

"Can you bring the salad out, hon?" Wendy calls. "And could you chill the wine? You should be wearing an apron. Look on the hook next to the stove."

Jeff's back is bent under the car hood. Blond hair slips over his bunched shoulders. In the right light, he looks like Sting in a news clip.

"Problems?" Allan says, peeping under the hood.

Jeff wipes the dipstick with a paper towel. He pulls on a rubber hose that sprouts from somewhere like a black tuber.

"Oil's low," he says. "And you should replace that hose. Can you figure why they put overhead cams in these things?"

"Nuts, eh?" Allan says. "Anyway, the steaks are almost up."

He puts his hand up to close the hood, but Jeff wedges his shoulders deeper inside to look at a fright-wig patch of wires. He tugs another hose.

"I've got one of those in my truck," he says. "You want me to get it?"

Allan wants to gun the engine until the radiator blows like something in a Mr. Magoo cartoon. Jeff is already half-way to his truck, where he'll root like a raccoon until he finds the right part.

Syl has sliced strawberries into little mouths and filled them with squirts of whipped cream. Now, she's arranging them in a motif around peeled purple grapes. Allan pinches one of the strawberries, but she slaps his fingers.

"Uh-uh," she says. "Wait till Mommy says it's ready."

When she laughs, her cheeks puff and her breasts move heavily under her baggy yellow shirt. He almost asks if she's pregnant, but roots in the refrigerator for the salad instead. The cream pitcher tips and slops light beige goo down the back wall. He chooses not to notice. He grabs beer from the rack and shuts the door quickly. He snaps the top off a can and takes several gulps before Syl can ask if he wants a glass.

"Steaks are nearly ready," he says. "You want me to carry that fruit plate? I can balance it on the salad bowl."

"I have to chill it first," she says, pushing past him.

She pauses and reads the Bizarro cartoon that's stuck to the fridge door with carrot-shaped magnets. Wendy put it up. It shows a woman carrying a striped container with Col. Sanders' picture on it. She's saying to her husband: "Children? I thought you said it's about time we had some chicken."

"You guys," Syl laughs. "Will you ever have kids?"

"Wendy," Allan shrugs, "prefers chicken."

Syl shakes her head. She opens the fridge door and bends over with a small whoof.

"Oh God, look, something's spilled here," she says. "Hand me the dish cloth will you, Allan? I'll wipe this up."

Allan goes outside cradling a dozen cans of beer in his arms along with the food, the forks and the knives.

He drains the wine into Jeff's glass and tosses the bottle over his shoulder. There's a muddy thud as it hits the lawn, then a clink as the neck bumps the back fence.

"Allan," Wendy says. "For Heaven's sake."

Syl giggles. She and Jeff hold hands below the arms of their patio chairs. Jeff grins. He leans across and kisses Syl on the cheek, then nibbles at the corner of her mouth. Allan opens two beer and pushes one across the table. The girls are drinking gin and tonics.

"What I'd give for the old days," Allan says. "This would be the perfect moment to roll a joint."

"I can't smoke anymore," Wendy says. "I just can't."

"We don't have any in the house, do we?" Allan asks.

"You know we don't," she says.

She rises to pick up the wine bottle, but he beats her to it. Bending over by the fence, he looks through the pickets hoping to catch a peek of Sherry Glenman changing in her bathroom. The Glenmans have a pool and were in swimming just as Allan and Wendy, Jeff and Syl, finished the barbecue.

But Sherry's already changed into deck clothes and is lying on a *chaise-longue* beside her husband. He's the principal at the school where Wendy teaches history. He wears a captain's hat all summer, even sometimes in the pool for comic effect. He waves Allan over for a drink.

"Later," Allan says, pointing at the patio. "Company."

He nearly heaves the wine bottle at the house just to see the glass burst like Walt Disney starlight around Wendy's neck and shoulders, across Syl's lap, down Jeff's back. He stops in the middle of the lawn. He nearly bursts out laughing.

Syl and Wendy are on to lettuce crispers. Allan says he'd love a smoke. He hasn't wanted one this much for ages.

"It puts me to sleep," Wendy says.

Syl nods. Jeff nuzzles her ear. Their wedding is set for October. Jeff will be Allan's brother-in-law. Jeff the mechanic, who knows an overhead cam from a muffler. Who checks Allan's oil.

"I got some dope," he says. "In the truck."

Allan pops another beer and pushes it across the table before he realizes Jeff hasn't half-finished the first one.

"Well, bring it out, my boy," he says. "The perfect end to a perfect evening."

He gulps his beer. Wendy and Syl pick up the cans from the table. With nothing to nuzzle or chew, Jeff disappears. He's back a few minutes later with a plastic baggie of pot.

"Is there anything you don't have in that truck?" Allan laughs. After one try at rolling the joint, his fingers are as nimble as a twenty-year-old's.

"Are the Glenmans outside?" Wendy says. "At least wait until they've gone in."

"Maybe we should go in," Syl says.

"Ridiculous," Allan says. "Is this 1968? Do the gendarmes still drive around sniffing the night air?"

He snuffles dog-like, leans over and pushes his nose up Wendy's bare arm. She giggles and grabs hair on the back of his head to make him stop.

"Besides," he says, tasting the small salt of her skin on his lips. "We're downwind."

He lights the joint and passes it to Wendy. She holds it between her fingertips like a squashed bug. Syl takes it and gives it to Jeff. He gives it back to Allan, who inhales and hands it to Wendy.

"Wanna another toke, babe?" he asks. "Dynamite shit."

Syl winces. Jeff laughs.

"Yuk," Wendy says. "Don't say babe, Allan. It's disgusting."

Then the girls go inside. When the door shuts behind them, the sound seems to come from four blocks away.

Allan opens the last beer. He slides Jeff's across the table and it hits the other two with a poomp. Jeff takes a sip of the first one. Allan sets his can on the table, then picks it up and takes another mouthful. Jeff stands up.

"I'm going in," he says. "See if Syl and Wendy need help."

Allan waves at him to sit down, swallows the mouthful of beer, mimes rolling another joint.

"How's the wedding plans coming?" he says. "You and Syl getting married. I still can't believe it. Just can't believe it."

He shakes his head. Jeff glances toward the back door. Smiles. Shrugs.

"I think we'll be happy," he says.

"Happy?" Allan says. "Of course you'll be happy. Before you know it, there'll be a little one in the house. Then before you know it, you'll be waking up at the crack of dawn to the sound of Saturday morning cartoons."

Jeff laughs. Says he'll probably be used to it by then after getting up for feedings. Diaper changings. Allan nods.

"Sure," he says. "Cartoons will be a reward after that stuff. I love cartoons myself. Bugs Bunny's my favourite. Even at college I watched Bugs Bunny. Just to relax, you know? Where'd you go to college, Jeff?"

Jeff says he was a mechanic's apprentice.

"Oh," Allan says. "Well, that's like college, isn't it? A lot more practical than the stuff I took I'll bet. Good old Bugs Bunny, though. Even in grad school, nothing relaxed me like Bugs."

He finishes his beer, reaches for one Jeff hasn't touched.

He sings: "Hold the chairs, the curtain lights, this is it, the night of nights…"

He bends forward, giggling.

"Overture," Jeff says.

"What?" Allan says.

"It's overtures," Jeff says. "Not 'hold the chairs.' The theme song. 'Overture, the curtain lights…'"

Allan leans back. Rubs his eyes.

"Did I say 'hold the chairs?'" he asks. "I must be more stoned than I thought."

But Jeff has already disappeared. The side door slams behind him as if someone has taken the house and moved it out to the lake.

"They're going," Wendy says.

In the summer dark, Allan can see only her hair framing her face and the cream-coloured sweater draped over her shoulders. The rest of his wife is geometric conclusions.

"Oh, no," he says. "So early?"

"It's midnight," she says. "Did you fall asleep?"

"I was looking for Andromeda," he says. "Seeking it out."

Wendy tells him to come and say goodnight. She touches her fingertips to his bald spot. She fusses with the barbecue, makes sure he's turned the burners off.

He stands and his knees go forward as if he's water-skiing. He stumbles sideways, catches his balance against her.

"Catch me now, I'm falling," he sings in a reedy voice. "The Kinks. 1971."

Or was it 1981? He swoops his hands under her skirt. She pushes the hem down, shoves him back with her free hand.

"Allan," she says. "You're getting carried away."

He takes a half-step back, tries to see her.

"Why do you always push like that?" he says.

She takes his hand. Tells him again to come and say goodnight.

Jeff has his arm around Syl's waist when Allan and Wendy come around the corner of the house. The newly-weds-to-be stand in the spill from the porch light.

"Don't give up your day job, Al," Syl says. "The singing, I mean."

Allan laughs, waggles his fingers at her as if brushing crumbs off a table. He invites them to have a liqueur.

"Tell us about your bun in the oven, Syl," he says.

"Don't be crude, Allan," Wendy says.

Jeff laughs. Says they have to go. Thanks them for everything. He moves off the step, tugging Syl.

"Whoop, the family man speaks," Allan hoots. "No dope in his truck soon."

Syl laughs. Wendy kisses them both on the cheeks. They're all in the driveway now. Allan can see the steering-wheel rim of Jeff's used Chev half-ton. It's in better shape than Allan's company Buick.

Allan mimes strumming a banjo and puts his lips close to Syl's ear. He sings: "Gonna tell you a story 'bout a man named Jed, a poor mountaineer barely kept his family."

"Allan," Wendy says. "Not so loud."

"God, he's singing again," Syl says. She tugs Jeff's arm. "Run away, run away."

"There she goes, folks," Allan hoots. "Now she's dragging him off. Pretty soon she'll be whupping him upside the head with a frying pan. Just like Granny whupping Jethro Clampet on *The Beverly Hillbillies.*"

He laughs. Syl laughs. Wendy laughs.

"Bodine," Jeff says.

Syl moves toward the truck. Wendy raises her left hand to wave goodbye. Allan stops laughing.

"Pardon me, Jeff?" he says.

Jeff slips his arm through Syl's and gives her waist a squeeze. They walk toward the truck.

"What did you say, Jeff?" Allan asks.

Jeff brushes his hair back from his face. Allan folds his arms across his chest. The porch spot light hitting the driveway turns everything cubic, rounded. Like they've all momentarily taken on the shape of the Milk Bottle in Monopoly.

"It was nothing, Al," Jeff says. "We gotta go."

"I asked what you said," Allan says. "And my name is Allan, not Al."

"Allan," Wendy says. "Don't be childish."

Jeff looks at her. Then rotates his neck as if that helps him believe where he is. When he speaks, his tone is painstaking.

"Bodine," he says. "Granny was a Clampet. Jed was a Clampet. Elly May was a Clampet. But Jethro was a Bodine. Pearl Bodine's son."

"Is that so?" Allan says. "A Bodine, eh? Well you know what you are, Jeff? You're a piss shit fuckhead. That's what you are."

He lurches forward, bringing his left fist around windmill-style. He points down the driveway. Syl looks at Wendy. Jeff looks at Wendy.

"Allan," Wendy says. "Apologize."

He looks at her. At the cream sweater draped over her shoulders. At the shadow angles of her body under the light summer shift.

"You," he says, "are a cunt."

"Hey," Syl says. "Come on, Allan. You don't talk to your wife that way. Come on. Apologize."

"Let's go," Jeff says. "He's loaded. Forget it. Come on, Syl. We'll see you later, Wendy."

Allan holds his breath until his pants feel loose around his waist.

"Get out of my driveway." He's shouting. "Get out of my neighbourhood."

Syl tries to put her arm around Wendy, but Jeff holds her and says something in her ear.

"I'll call you," Syl says to Wendy. "It'll be all right."

"Cunt-ca-cunt-cunt," Allan calls.

Then he runs. Sprints to the rear of the house and digs the wine bottle from the garbage. Coming back down the driveway, he's a kid again, racing across a fence top. Crouched, head up, hands out for balance. Each footfall a gamble.

He lobs the bottle as hard as he can. It smacks the pickup box just as Jeff pulls away. Explodes. Lights go on in the Glenmanths bedroom.

"Ha-ha," Allan laughs. "Ha-ha-ha-ha."

Jeff's tires squeal. He gets out and stands in the thin, warm light spilling from the cab. He picks up the jagged bottle neck.

"Pretty dumb, Al," he says, dropping it again.

Glass tinkles. Syl leans across the seat.

Allan's face shines when he turns to look up the driveway. The cream sweater is bunched now in his wife's hands. It will be wrinkled, ruined, if she stands there holding it all night. He weaves slightly, blinks at the porch light shining into his eyes.

He raises one foot, a few inches from the asphalt. Balances briefly on one leg. Small rocks pop beneath his shoe when he brings the foot down. He raises the other foot. Waits for Wendy to speak.

Calls

Breikreutz is turning off Ste. Catherine when he sees the man in the wheelchair. At first, he thinks the man is cradling a telephone receiver against one shoulder and holding a cheroot at waist-level in the other hand. He is three steps down Drummond before he sees the man is peeing on the sidewalk. The cheroot is really a stubby brown penis. The telephone is a spastic neck that locks the head sideways and down.

The head flops back, bobs to the far shoulder. One arm snaps upward. The eyes follow involuntarily. The hand grips a cup of panhandled quarters. The man's worn black leather jacket is zippered up to his chin.

Breikreutz steps over the sheet of pee. He drops a quarter in the cup.

"Nature calls, eh pal?" he says.

"Nuuhhh," the man says. "Nuhhhhh."

At the door of the Hotel Europa, a heavy woman with cropped, black hair brushes past. He stops, looks quickly back at her. But both she and wheelchair man have already disappeared into the harsh sunlight flooding the street.

In the Europa lobby, the wooden stools at the semi-circle corner bar are empty. A family of Salvadoran refugees sit on straight-backed chairs near the window looking out on Drummond. The father smokes a cigarette and watches the street. The teenaged children watch their father. The mother brings her hand up to touch two silver barrettes that hold her high-swept hair in place.

Breikreutz feels the quarter between his fingers. He wants to go over and perform a magician's trick with it for the girl. Make it disappear. Discover it in her ear, her palm. But he doesn't know how to do coin tricks. How to make things go away and reappear somewhere new.

He goes to the payphones and dials Lea-Anne. As he waits

for her service to answer, he looks through the doorway into the darkened salon that was once the Europa's crystal ballroom. In the shadows, he can see the broken chairs, the tables with legs snapped off leaning against walls. It's as if someone has arranged time itself recklessly around the room. The woman at the answering service says Lea-Anne can't be reached.

He was lying on the bed in Lea-Anne's studio apartment just across Sherbrooke Street from Parc Lafontaine. Across the room was the tan naugahyde couch where the heavy-set woman lay wrapped in a blanket that time. He saw only her dark hair and her fingers pulling the blanket over her shoulders.

Lea-Anne sat on the side of the bed, fluffed her blonde hair with her fingers. She had to make a call. She was conscientious about checking in, following up. Breikreutz told her once if she just learned how to bargain she could be in sales. She said she already was. And that she never bargained.

That was why she could afford another place up in Notre-Dame-de-Grace. She cabbed it downtown after supper and back again when the bars closed. She never took customers there, never told them about it, but Breikreutz had followed her one night from the Queen Elizabeth Hotel. All the way out Sherbrooke.

"You mind if I make this call?" she asked, cradling the receiver between her cheek and shoulder. "Some guys do when it's still their time."

He shrugged, waved. He didn't mind anything she did. If he did, he wouldn't have been one of her regulars. That's what she called him—a regular. He liked the sound of that. Regular.

"Fuck," Lea-Anne said.

She looked at a number, recognizing it. She started to dial, hung up. Pressed the receiver down as if it would spring up if she let go too fast. She crossed the studio and sat naked on the tan couch, staring at the number. When she looked up, she seemed startled Breikreutz was still there.

"Problems?" he said.

"This guy," Lea-Anne said. "A guy."

"A guy," Breikreutz said.

"He wants me to call him," she said.

"Pimp?" Breikreutz said.

Lea-Anne shook her head. Some guy with Air Canada. Staying at the Queen Elizabeth.

She got up slowly, walked back toward the bed, crumbled the paper and tossed it onto the bureau. Her small breasts jiggled. A silver thread stuck to her blond pubic hair.

"I went with him once before," she said. "He was drunk. Really drunk. He kept telling me how bad he needed me. I shouldn't have gone to his room, but he offered me 200 bucks."

"What did he do?" Brei kreutz asked. "Pull a knife?"

She'd told him men sometimes did. The weird ones usually just asked her to pee on them. But sometimes they pulled knives. Made her talk her way out of it.

"No," she said. "Not on me. On himself. He pulled a knife on himself."

She smoothed the paper, crumpled it again.

"He went in the can. He was in there so long, I started thinking maybe he was having a heart attack or something. This big fat guy had a heart attack on me once. Right on top of me. I couldn't get out from underneath him. I've never been so scared in my life.

"Anyway this guy the other night, he was in the can so long I finally knocked on the door. I thought he was either gassed out or dead. I go 'are you all right in there?' I hear this 'nuhhhh' sound. I push open the door. He's sitting on the can with his legs spread and there's blood dripping from his, you know, sac.

"I go 'what the hell are you doing?' He's got this little knife, it's like a nail file except it's got sharp edges on both sides. And he's cut himself open with it. He's bleeding all over the place. All over himself.

"He starts crying. He's sitting on the can crying and bleeding and he says to me 'I don't deserve to have a dick.' I see these scars all over. He's done this before, you know?"

"Anyway, I say 'thank-you very much, I'll be leaving now.' But he starts crying even harder and telling me I'm the only one who can make him feel like a man. Begging me to stay. There's blood all over the place. All over the place."

"Jesus," Breikreutz said. "Jesus God."

He is raising the forkful of steak tartar to his lips in the Bistro St. Denis when he sees the older woman's hand moving in small circles on the younger woman's back. The women sit on high stools at the bar and he can see only the left profile of one, the right profile of the other. But he recognizes the motion, the intent, of the kneading fingers. The woman being touched reaches for a quarter from the other's free hand.

The panic was there on the second call. He heard it before Lea-Anne grabbed the receiver and motioned she wanted privacy.

She was in the bathroom cleaning up when the first call came. Breikreutz picked up the phone reflexively. He was relieved when a voice asked for Sherry.

"You've got the wrong number," Breikreutz said. "There's no Sherry here."

There was harsh, nasal breath on the other end, then a man reciting Lea-Anne's number.

"Let me speak to Sherry," the caller said.

Breikreutz hung up. Jumped when the phone rang again.

"I know she's there—I fucking-well followed her," the

caller said.

It was the same voice. The same man. But this time, there was panic, sharp as wire filaments snagging Breikreutz's ear.

Before he could answer, Lea-Anne came out of the bathroom in her underwear. She listened, rolled her eyes, waved at Breikreutz to wait. He went into the bathroom and washed his hands. When he came out, she was dressed, sitting on the tan couch, smoking.

"He asked for someone named Sherry," he said.

"So?" she said. "So what?"

The way she spoke, he didn't need to ask if the caller was the man with the scars. She turned away when Breikreutz asked how she'd possibly seen those scars through all that blood.

When Breikreutz looks up, the younger woman is disappearing through a door that leads to the Bistro's basement. There are payphones down there, and a service entrance. Her companion speaks loud, excited French to the waiter behind the bar. Runs her fingers repeatedly through her cropped black hair. Breikreutz recognizes her as the woman on the couch in Lea-Anne's apartment. The woman at the window of the house in NDG. The forkful of raw steak goes putrid in his mouth.

He opened the driver's door and stepped out, calling to her across the roof. He was surprised how easily he'd found his way from the time he'd followed her. He remembered the cab beating it across traffic on Sherbrooke at the Himalaya Temple Restaurant and going the wrong way up Northcliffe.

"Lea-Anne," he said.

She took three steps up the walk before turning. He said her name again. Sherry. She'd removed her makeup in the cab, or in a washroom somewhere. Her face, at the rim of the streetlight, was chalk.

"It's me," he said. "Breikreutz."

She moved her left shoulder forward slightly and then up into a brief shrug. The motion drew Breikreutz's eyes and he noticed the curtains in the window behind her were parted. He could see a woman looking out.

"Do I know you?" Lea-Anne asked. "You're not a cop are you?"

"Lea-Anne," Breikreutz said. "It's Breikreutz. The regular."

She squinted. He could feel the woman at the curtains without even looking up.

"Oh," Lea-Anne said. "Oh yeah. I didn't recognize you for a minute. In the dark, I mean. Look, I'm not working, okay? I'm finished for tonight. Call me tomorrow."

He took a careful step away from the car. Told her he didn't want that. He just wanted to talk. Five minutes. Her shoulder was pulling toward the window. She was struggling not to look.

"I want to talk about that guy," he said. "The one you told me about."

"A guy?" she said. "You want to talk to me about a guy?"

"The one with the knife," he said. "Who cut himself."

She didn't know what he meant. Asked if he was sure they knew each other.

"He called your place on Sherbrooke when I was there," Breikreutz said. "Twice. Remember?"

"Oh," Lea-Anne said. "Him."

Breikreutz drains his wine and signals the waiter for another. He's chewing bread when the younger woman re-appears and resumes her seat at the bar. The other woman's hand begins circling again, rising up the blouse toward the blonde hair. At the shoulder, its fingers dig into the blue cotton, puckering the fabric.

He's seen that hand pulling a blanket over a turned shoulder. Seen it let a curtain fall across the window of Lea-Anne's house.

He edged himself through the darkness to the front of the car. He leaned against the hood a few feet from Lea-Anne. He kept eye contact across the darkness. Kept his voice soft. Kept her talking. He was sure if he made a single sudden move, the woman watching would act. He didn't know how.

"He pays you to watch him, doesn't he?" Breikreutz asked.

"No," Lea-Anne said. "He pays me for a good time. Just like you do."

"But you feed it," he told her. "If you refused, he'd stop."

"Maybe," Lea-Anne said. "So?"

In the lobby of the Europa, he pounds for service on the semi-circle bar before he realizes it's closed. Only the chairs by the window are open. Empty, it's obvious they've been brought from a formal dining-room somewhere. That they've been placed near the lobby window because there's no use for them where they belong. Because the place they belong no longer exists.

"Cab," he calls to the nightclerk. "Waiting for a cab."

The clerk retreats, leaving Breikreutz alone. He sits in one of the window chairs, tries to remember the names of the bars he's been in. He looks out, hopes he'll see the wheelchair man taking another pee. The street's as empty as the lobby.

He wonders where the man sleeps at night. He wonders who stills those waving arms and bends them into the soft, worn sleeves every morning? He wonders who tells refugees when it's time to run.

He's come back to the Europa believing the refugee woman would still be there. Thinking she would be sitting by the window, reaching up, in the out-of-place chair.

He wanted to admire the silver barrettes in her high, dark hair. Wanted to tell her how he admired her for escaping. Ask how she did it. Discover her skills. He can't even remember when he decided to come back. Realizes she was probably already gone.

He holds a quarter in his palm. Around the corner at the payphones, he dials.

The humidity, in the darkness, felt cumulus under the over-hanging maples. It dripped down his neck. It swirled, in the streetlight, like moths.

"You can't keep doing it to him," he told Lea-Anne. "It's not right."

She balanced, almost comically, on her high heels. Her face, leaning forward, was bleach.

"What's it got to do with you?" she asked. "What makes it your fucking business anyway?"

The merest movement of the muscles in his thighs made her break. The slightest push forward from the hood of the car made her turn, wobbling on her heels.

The switchboard operator at the Queen Elizabeth makes things difficult. She can't give out names. He controls his tongue.

"Waverly," he says. "Mr. Waverly. With Air Canada."

They have no Waverlys.

"Listen," Breikreutz says. "I have to contact him. His son's been killed. Richard. Richard's been killed."

He's wonders if she hears the lie. She goes off the line. He goes into limbo.

"We have a Mr. Dalton with Air Canada," she says when she comes back on.

"Mr. Dalton," Breikreutz says. "Put me through. Please."

When Mr. Dalton finally answers he sounds as drunk as Breikreutz feels. But it's the same voice. The same man who called Lea-Anne's asking for Sherry.

"Who's calling?" Mr. Dalton says.

"Mr. Dalton, I know I sound drunk," Breikreutz says. "Pissed. I know that. I am pissed. I know that. Is Lea-Anne there now, Mr. Dalton?"

"You've got the wrong room, pal," Mr. Dalton says. "There's no Lea-Anne here."

"Mr. Dalton," Breikreutz says. "I recognize your voice. You called Lea-Anne's apartment twice, remember? I have to talk to you, Mr. Dalton."

Breikreutz hears music—a radio—in the background. But no voices. He wonders if Mr. Dalton is waving a hand at someone to be quiet. He wonders what Mr. Dalton is holding in his hand.

"Mr. Dalton, please don't hang up," Breikreutz says. "She's told me about you, Mr. Dalton. I know."

He hears Mr. Dalton's harsh breath. He wants to tell Mr. Dalton that Sherry is Lea-Anne. Lea-Anne is Sherry. He wants to tell Mr. Dalton about the woman who watches. He wants to tell him to get away. Escape. Run. Just run.

The phone goes dead against his ear.

Breikreutz saw Lea-Anne for the last time when she turned. Saw her face at the moment when she couldn't resist any longer. At the moment her eyes looked involuntarily at the window. Before she reached the steps, the curtain was drawn.

He listens, now, to the emptiness of the Europa lobby. The emptiness of the street. Of the receiver pressed against his ear. He dials Lea-Anne one last time.

Waiting for the service to answer, he remembers how the woman's cropped, black hair disappeared as Lea-Anne

37

reached the steps.

Vanished. The way the refugee woman and her family would have suddenly vanished from their neighbours. The way the leather-jacket man and his wheelchair vanished from the street. The way Mr. Dalton wants to vanish from himself. She reappeared at the Bistro, like the magician's coin, touching someone new with those hands.

Then he realizes she was here at the Europa, too. She was at the door the time he saw the cripple pissing in the street. The time he saw the refugee woman reaching for the silver in her hair. The first time he tried to reach Lea-Anne after the night outside the house in NDG.

The service says Lea-Anne still can't be reached. Her number's been disconnected.

He leans against the phone. He cannot remember when he last slept. He cannot do anything else, now, but stare through the doorway of the old ballroom. Staring, drunk, exhausted, he's suddenly sure the watching woman was more than merely the magician's coin. He's convinced she was here arranging something that day. Arranging everything that's happened since. That even the illusion of escape belonged to her.

Somehow, he moves. Takes a few steps across the worn carpet to the entrance of the ruined salon where he stares. Stares into the darkness until the broken furniture begins to shift, change, become almost fluid.

He stares until the snapped tables, the abandoned chairs, assume the forms of the angled limbs of those who danced here very long ago. As they would have danced at the opening gala on New Year's Eve, 1920.

White-gloved waiters carry silver salvers of spiced meats, of golden champagne. The ladies' silken gowns are stunning, their bare arms so smooth. Hands rest gently on partners' shoulders, fingers spread slightly on backs, as graceful couples waltz. As they turn and swirl. As the bright crowd streams past, calling out his name.

Harsh voices warn this is more of the watching woman's work, another of her creations. He doesn't care.

The coast is clear. He steps inside.

SARA MCDONALD

jenny's IUD is picking up signals from outer space

Jenny is going to be famous one day, you can tell just by looking at her. It's hard to say what she might be famous for because just being Jenny should be enough. I'm keeping notes and one day I'll write the story of her life. The best parts are the ones she makes up.

Jenny has forgotten how to sleep. It used to be so easy, she says. I never even had to think about it. Since she started thinking about it she can't do it anymore. It's like swimming, she says. When she thinks about the water holding her up she always sinks. She won't ride in airplanes because she believes the main cause of crashes is people who can't believe the air will hold them up.

Jenny lets men in bars buy her drinks. When I tell her that they are going to expect something she just laughs and says that's their problem. Jenny and I always dance the last dance together and walk out of the bar arm in arm.

Jenny is getting her life together, bit by bit. She says it's like doing a jigsaw puzzle only without the picture on the box to go by.

Jenny used to have a family like everybody else but she claims to have misplaced them. She says when she was twelve the family was moving cross-country with a truck and a U-Haul, and they forgot her at a gas station when they were on a bathroom break. Jenny doesn't hold a grudge about this, she says when they realized she wasn't in the back they probably turned around and came back for her. Thing is, by that time she'd already gotten into somebody else's car.

Jenny and I live in a women's commune, no men allowed. Some of the other straight women here have been known to sneak the occasional guy into their rooms but Jenny plays by the rules. She's slept with guys in the Lorass bin out back a couple of times though, and says it's better that way because you don't have to worry about them wanting to spend the night.

Jenny can sing like Bessie Smith when she's drunk. I tell her that she should be a singer and go on the road but she says it would turn her into an alcoholic. She can't sing when she's sober; she opens her mouth and nothing comes out.

Jenny used to read Tarot cards but once she saw a death in the cards that came true so she stopped. She always knows what is going to happen next; sometimes she tells me and sometimes she doesn't. She's my guardian angel and lets me know on days when it's best not to go out of the house. On these days we stay in bed and eat jam sandwiches and make up stories for each other.

Jenny has a fear of electrical appliances. She won't use the stove or curl her hair with a curling-iron or vacuum even when it's her turn. She thinks that she was electrocuted in a previous life. She even thinks she might have gotten the chair for something.

Jenny doesn't do anything for a living and I don't know where her money comes from. Every month's end when I ask if she's going to be able to make rent she says: the universe will provide. I'm not sure what this means. It could mean that she rides the subway at rush hour and picks people's pockets. I don't ask.

43

Jenny used to work as an artist's model and pose in the nude. I think she is the most beautiful woman I have ever known. She likes being naked and walks around the house that way sometimes. Some of the other women in the commune complain about it but I think it's like a gift Jenny has, she can be naked better than anybody I know. She has scars all over her torso but she won't say how she got them and sometimes I have nightmares about them.

Jenny gets thrown out of museums and gallerys for caressing the sculptures. You have to feel them, she says. You have to pretend you're blind. Once she got caught licking a painting to see how it tasted.

Jenny is never bored; she says she tried it once and didn't like it. She is always thinking about something and if you ask her she'll tell you what it is. I try not to ask too often because that would spoil it, so I wait until she's being real quiet and has a funny look on her face. Then she'll tell me things like: Bette Davis' grandson stuck a peanut up his nose and lost 30% of his hearing. One time she told me that she'd connected all the moles on her stomach and they made a fish.

Jenny makes lists all the time and leaves them all over the house for anybody to see. Sometimes they don't say anything interesting, just junk like: water the fern, buy tampons, get a haircut. Other times they are lists of people she's slept with, or means to write letters to, or thinks she was in past lives. Once I found a piece of paper that said things to do in big letters across the top and underneath she had written: tell Janna that I love her. She never did but the next day the list was still there with its single entry crossed off, so I guess she figured I already knew.

Jenny is the kind of person that things happen to. Strange things. She says that she used to walk around with a victim sign on her back, but doesn't anymore. She's seen more flashers than anyone I know. She sees ghosts too, and one time she told me that her IUD was picking up signals from outer space again. Jenny thought she was losing her mind one time. She was in a public washroom and staring at all the faces in the mirror above the sinks and couldn't figure out which one was hers. Maybe this never happened to her, she says. Maybe she only saw it in a movie, but it's still a bad sign.

Jenny talks about getting out, moving somewhere new and starting over. I go real quiet when she talks likes this because I don't want her to ever leave. Sometimes, even with other people I feel like I'm alone in the room, but never with Jenny. She's one of those people who can hear you even when you're not talking.

the rosetta stone

Two Mormons or Jehovahs, or whoever those guys with the haircuts are, came to my door this morning.

"We're here to talk to God about you," said the younger one, blushing and stammering.

"Talk to you about God," corrected the older one.

I didn't say anything and they just stood there and stared at me like a pair of idiots. Finally the older guy spoke up: "Wouldn't you like to put some clothes on?" he asked.

"Yes," I said, and closed the door. But I didn't.

I took a polaroid of myself naked and pasted it into the book. The book is like a day-by-day record of my life with different things pasted in. There's a whole row of them on my shelf in no particular order, because I've never been much of a linear thinker. They're full of polaroids, pages out of books I was reading at the time, pieces of my hair from each time it's changed colour, power bills I didn't feel like paying, burnt matches, broken shoelaces, newspaper horoscopes, orange peels and other items of particular significance. I like to think of it as an autobiographical novel for illiterates, or people just too lazy to read.

I got one of those "Make Your Own Will" kits from Coles and wrote up that all the volumes are to go the British Museum when I die. I like to think of it there in the same building with James Joyce's manuscripts, and the Rosetta Stone, and the crumbling mummies, and the toilet paper in the loo with "Property of Her Majesty the Queen" stamped on every square. I like to think of the tourists and the existentialists sitting in the cafeteria there, drinking watery tea and discussing it. Using words like: symbolism, relevance—and ambiguity.

My friend Richard phoned just as I was writing down the date underneath the fresh polaroid of myself. Richard likes to check up on me every once in awhile.

"Are you still crazy?" he asked me.

"I don't really know, Richard," I said. "It's kind of hard to tell from the inside."

"I guess it would be," he said. "Why don't you tell me about what you did today?"

So I told him that two guys saw me naked and wanted to talk to God about it.

"I guess you're still crazy," said Richard.

"Well, if you say so."

After that the conversation pretty much went downhill. I didn't bother to tell Richard about the diaries I've been keeping. He's such a bloody know-it-all sometimes, and talks down to me like I don't know anything. The thing is, I bet you Richard has never even seen the Rosetta Stone.

some days I wake up missing everybody

I

I was walking to the library, wearing colours to match the sky and daring it to rain, and I started to follow a man I thought was you and knew wasn't. He was wearing the sort of hat I imagined you would wear in this sort of weather (I'd never known you in this sort of weather), and he was swinging his long arms at his sides. He was staring at the legs of the women passing by him, and perhaps it was this more than anything that made me think him you. As the man who wasn't you was outdistancing me with his familiar lanky walk I ran into a man I did know, or had known, and my arms went out to him before I remembered he'd known me before I was in the habit of hugging and getting close enough to hear the reassurance of a heartbeat. Over his shoulder I could just see your hat, bobbing to some unheard song, above the heads of the everyday strangers.

2

Everything reminds me of you. The other night driving home from the bar with a friend, she stopped the car and said: last time that moon was full you two were together. She knows all about the empty mailbox and the phone I will to ring. We both try to think more of the full moon and less of the empty bed. Of course there are others, there have always been others, but there are certain things the heart will not allow. But no, I will not speak of the heart here. Or love. Love for me in this city is a man who calls and weeps about loss. I don't know what it means in the city where you now sleep.

3

I was late for the poetry reading and had to take a seat at the back. The poet had already begun, he was reading a poem I used to know, one that you used to read to me. I had to resist standing up and stopping the poet because he wasn't reading the poem right. The way he turned a phrase was not the way you would, and the resonance was wrong. There are certain words I can hear only in your voice. There was a man sitting some ten rows down from me and it suddenly occurred to me that he was you. He was balding, the dome of his skull pink and shiny. When I last saw you, you still had all your hair. I wanted to cry for the sight of your poor head, so naked and vulnerable. I couldn't hear the poet any longer because I was thinking of what pain we once brought each other as we were grasping for joy.

4

In the single photo I have of you the shadows deform you, obscure the lines of your face, make of you someone I never knew. The man I remember, whose memory I call up in darkened rooms and solitary hours, is someone you might—given the opportunity—deny the existence of. I was never that man, you might say with cruel certainty. There are no pictures in my mind of you with somebody else. All day I have been thinking that you are thinking of me. I am embarrassed by my need, uncertain of my role. At the age of five I vowed never to be a wife, at twenty never a mistress. That was when I still saw things in black and white. Before I knew anything of Ansel Adams and his bloody seven zones of grey necessary to a good picture.

5

Some days I wake up missing everybody I've ever known and everybody I've never met; other days I think that to have loved so many is never to have truly loved at all. If I say that I miss you, you must understand what I mean, which I can define only by what I don't mean: I don't want you back. I enjoy missing you. When I say *you* I mean all the men I ever left or who left me or who chance never allowed me to meet. When I say *I,* I mean of course *she* a character of my own invention. None of this has anything to do with me. Does this make a difference? Of course not. Any man I've ever known can search these pages for evidence of betrayal. There are secrets I will never tell; I could illustrate with an example, but I won't. I cannot say if I am motivated by kindness or merely caution. Maybe none of this is real; maybe the only one I truly miss is also a character of my own invention.

all I ever wanted was the moon

I

I asked him if he would stay the night. It's sort of nice sometimes to wake up with your arm all pins and needles from
being beneath someone's head all night long.

"I can't," he said.

"Just sleep, I mean. That's all."

"I know," he said. "But I still can't."

Tom and I had a relationship based on give and take; I gave
and he took. We had all kinds of unspoken agreements, like
that I wouldn't phone him at home and he wouldn't show me
pictures of his kids.

"Tea?" I asked. He nodded and I went into the kitchen to
put the kettle on. When I came back he was pacing in circles
around my small living-room and staring at the pictures on
the walls like he'd never seen them before. His hand went up
to stroke the beard he'd shaved off months before.

"Jacquie and I—" he said.

I'd always wondered what she looked like, and if maybe she
looked a little like me, or I like her. I'd found short red hairs on
Tom's clothes a few times and when I asked him if he owned an
Irish Setter he'd said no. I wondered other things about her
too. If I might have liked her if we had met by chance, at the
foreign film night at the library for example, and shared a coffee afterwards. If we might have found a common bond like
that we both had divorced parents, or thought that wearing
black made us look thin, or that we both liked the same type of
man. And maybe after we'd sat through however many Fellini
or Godard films together, and shared however many coffees or
even cappucinos, maybe after all that shared experience she
would have said: You really must come by for supper some
evening and meet my husband and the kids. And maybe I

would have gone.

It's hard not to be angry with Tom for denying me this as well. A friendship between women is one of those things that can carry you through adolesence and menopause and other bad days.

"Sorry, I wasn't listening," I said, and walked past Tom into the kitchen. I started getting the tea things out and clattering cups into saucers.

"Ruth," he said. He touched me softly from behind, his hand tentatively circling the space between my shoulder-blades; the buds of my wings my mother called them when I was young.

"I said that Jacquie and I are going away for awhile and we're going to try and make things work."

I wondered if he called her Jacquie when they made love or simply luv as he did me.

"I told her about us," he said. "I promised her it's over."

"I know," I said. And the kettle began to whistle so I made the tea.

2

I was having coffee in the Starlight Café down the street from my place one night about a week after Tom left. It was the first time I'd been out of the house since I'd dyed my hair red. I'd spent the weekend at home staring at myself in the mirror and thinking: now what did you want to go and do a thing like that for? The thought kept coming out in my mother's voice.

I was checking out my reflection in the bowl of my spoon when I noticed this guy in the next booth. He was talking to himself and maybe that was what I noticed first, or maybe it was that he was good looking and alone, or maybe it was the streak of white in his hair that made me think of Holden Caulfield.

The chinese waiter, coffee pot in one hand and menus in the other kept passing by Holden who would stare forlornly after him. I picked out his voice from the backgound clatter of the café—and he was saying: May I have a cup of coffee, please. He kept shifting the emphasis from word to word like an actor rehearsing a line. I picked up my coffee cup and slid into the seat across from him. I held up my cup and the waiter came over and gave us both refills.

"Thanks," said Holden and smiled. A rueful, little boy smile. God save me from the little boy men.

His real name was Homer. He had to tell me three times before I believed him. He said that his father was a Greek Classicist.

When I woke up in the morning it was with his arm beneath my head. He was awake and smiling at me.

"I can't sleep in strange places," he said.

It was nice to wake up with somebody again, even with Tom he hardly ever stayed straight through until morning. I wasn't over Tom though, and the way I could tell was I kept looking for the ways that Homer's body differed from his. Tom was a big solid sort of man and Homer was built more like me, skinny and sparrow-boned.

"I'll get breakfast," Homer said. "You stay right where you are." He pulled on his clothes and backed out of the bedroom. I thought I'd died and gone to heaven until I heard the slam of the front door. Well that's that, I thought. Nothing sloppy or sentimental about that one.

An hour later he showed up with two suitcases.

"Back into bed," he said. "You weren't supposed to get up." He dumped the contents of one of the suitcases onto my bed, spilling out an assortment of stuffed animals and an espresso maker. He stashed the espresso maker under his arm and headed for the kitchen. I grabbed a penguin that had landed near my feet and nestled under the covers with it.

"Make yourself at home," I told it.

3

The first thing Liz asked me at lunch the next day was why in the hell I had dyed my hair red.

"I was depressed," I said. "I thought it might cheer me up."

"Well I don't like it; you don't look like you anymore."

"I think that was the general idea," I said.

Liz and I both worked for the same corporation and we had lunch together every day. This was looked on with suspicion and disapproval by our co-workers because I was a lowly clerk steno while Liz was upper management. I didn't mind being shunned by the other clerk stenos though because I'd found them to be a pretty narrow-minded lot. I was never able to hold up my end in conversations about things like recipes for light morning coffee cake.

"So who's the new guy?" asked Liz.

"How do you know there is one?"

"You've got that way of moving back again, like your bones are made of jello or something. You're only that way when you're getting it," Liz said.

"You're right," I said. "There might be somebody new, but it's still too early to tell."

Liz was my best friend in the world, but I didn't know how to tell her that a week after the supposed love of my life had walked out on me I had taken up with an out of work actor named Homer. Liz has her life together; she has a house and a husband and all those things that everybody is supposed to want.

"Fine," she said. "Don't tell me who it is then. I just hope he's helping you get over that shit Tom. No lectures I promise. Just tell me you're happy."

"You know how in movies, love stories I mean, there's always that scene midway through where it's like holding hands and smiling at the balloon man and all that hokey stuff. Where about a week passes in three minutes and everything's happening real fast and in time with some horribly significant background music."

"Yeah," said Liz. "The one that's like the MTV version of your life, or maybe somebody else's life."

"Right," I said. "That's what I'm waiting for."

"Poor baby," she said. "You really want it all, don't you?"

4

Homer never went home again after that first morning; he became just another part of my daily routine very quickly. He would be up before I was in the morning and I would wake to the smell of coffee brewing, and when I got home at the end of a day dinner would be on the table. It was like having a wife.

About a week after he came to stay I got home from work one day and there was no dinner on the table. Homer was sitting in the dark on the couch, pouting.

"You got a letter today," he said and handed me a postcard. It was one of those gag cards where instead of a picture it's just black and then says in white lettering at the bottom: Toronto at night. On the back was scrawled: wish you were here.

"It must be somebody's idea of a joke," I told Homer. I threw it in the garbage and went to sit beside him on the couch.

"Quit your job," Homer said. "You shouldn't be typing somebody's crummy letters all day long. You were meant to lie on a *chaise-longue* and have somebody feed you grapes. How can you stoop so low as to be a goddamn secretary?"

"It pays the rent," I said.

"Quit. Come away with me. We could go anywhere; we could be anybody."

"Slow down," I said. "We've only known each other a week. What makes you think you know me?"

"Well," he looked around the room. "You like old things, some people might even call it junk."

I hit him with a pillow embroidered with the slogan *Souvenir of Niagara Falls*.

"But I like this place," he said. "It feels like a home, like somebody real lives here. I like that," he pointed at an empty wooden picture frame hanging on the wall. "It makes a statement about art, about minimalism, about the human condition—"

"It's an empty picture frame. I didn't like the picture so I threw it away."

I moved into his lap and pressed my face into his neck.

"Have you ever thought of growing a beard?" I asked.

When Homer was asleep I snuck into the kitchen and rummaged through the garbage until I found the postcard. Bits of potato peels and coffee grounds were stuck to it.

I had to go through all the cupboards to find the teapot. Homer only drank espresso so that was what I'd been drinking too.

The kitchen window reflected myself back at me, shutting out the night. I was paler than usual and my newly dyed red hair made me look kind of freaky.

The card was postmarked Toronto.

He missed me.

But not enough to give a return address.

5

I never knew what Homer did in the hours when I was at work and I never really questioned it either. He was like the fridge light, you shut the door and assumed it went off but you never really knew for sure. Homer was one of those people who never gave any sign of having a past, he simply appeared when I needed him.

His life was contained in the second suitcase that sat at the foot of my bed where he'd dropped it the morning he made me breakfast. Things appeared from it and disappeared back into it for the first week or so. Then, one morning before I left for work I emptied a bureau drawer and cleared out some space in the closet. When I got home the suitcase was gone, and neither of us said anything about it. This was as close as we could come to commitment.

Then, just when life was starting to seem normal the call finally came, just when I'd finally stopped expecting it.

"I miss you," he said, before even saying my name.

He just assumed I would answer the phone, that there wouldn't be anybody else here. What if Homer had answered?

"Ruth? Are you there?" he asked when I didn't answer.

"Yes," I said. "I'm here. Where are you?"

"Toronto," he said. "Will you come?"

"The next plane." He gave me the name of a hotel to meet him at.

"Bye luv," he said and hung up before I could ask any of the wrong questions.

Homer came home with take-out Chinese while I was packing. I'd sort of forgotten about him and hadn't thought up anything to say. He just looked at me like I was someone he didn't know and then set the food down on the bureau and started to help me fold my clothes.

"How long will you be gone?" he asked. Not where or who

with.

"I'm not sure," I said.

He put the last of my clothes into the suitcase and shut it. His lips were drawn tight as he snapped the locks.

"I can drive you to the airport," he said.

"I already called a cab. Thanks."

"You're shaking," he said. He drew me to him and held me tight until my breathing started to slow.

"C'mon now." He pulled back a little so that I had to look at him. "Do you want me here when you get back?"

"Yes," I said, then: "It's up to you."

6

I knew that Tom wouldn't be there to meet my plane but caught myself scanning the crowds for the silly hat he wore season after season. He wasn't there of course.

The girl who'd shared a seat with me on the plane, and who had occupied her time painting her nails a putrid shade of peach, was now waving her hands frantically in the air. Then above the heads of the crowd I saw an answering pair of waving hands. A man pushed through the crowd, scooped her up like a child and swung her gleefully through the air. Her skirt swirled about, up and over her head and when her face re-emerged she was laughing almost crying.

They stood there holding hands while the luggage circled past them and every so often she would look up at him as if amazed that he was still there.

I grabbed my suitcase and fled to the nearest washroom. I ran the water as cold as I could get it and then splashed it all over my face, drenching my clothes in the process. My mascara ran down my cheeks and my hair clung to my face like seaweed. The face I'd so carefully put on for Tom was gone, my makeup was in my purse and I could have started over, but instead I scrubbed my face dry with a paper towel until it was red and chapped.

I caught the bus that was going downtown to the hotels and was suddenly afraid that I'd got the name of the hotel wrong. Everytime the driver would call out a stop I would run the name over in my mind to see if it sounded familiar. Finally he called out one that I was sure of and I got off.

When I got into the hotel I realized I didn't know whose name we'd be booked under. The first thing I did was to head for the gift shop and buy a pack of cigarettes. I hadn't smoked for nearly three years but it seemed like a good time to start.

I sat down on one of the plush lobby couches and lit a cigarette to help me think. I watched the people spinning through the revolving doors: lots of people in swanky clothes whizzed by, all of them obviously with a set destination. This was not a hotel for strays and wanderers.

I butted out my cigarette and strode purposefully over to the desk. Anyone watching me would think I knew where I was going.

"I have a reservation," I said to the desk clerk. "I believe the name is Armstrong," I said in a slightly firmer voice. He looked at me kind of funny but keyed the name into his computer, then smiled at me.

"Is your husband with you, Mrs. Armstrong?"

"He'll be joining me later," I said and took the paper he shoved across the desk to me. Mrs. Armstrong I signed in a peculiar backslant. I finished the signature with a flourish that was supposed to underscore the name but ended up cutting cleanly through it.

Once I got in the room I found that I couldn't sit down. I put my suitcase down at the foot of the bed and looking at it there made me think of Homer. I pulled back the drapes, forced the windows open and looked out on the street: more strangers whizzing by. Lots of men in hats, but none of them were Tom.

I kept emptying the ashtrays so that when he arrived he wouldn't think I'd been chain smoking, pacing and worrying, which was exactly what I was doing. I thought of leaving and coming back; I thought of leaving and not coming back. I thought of taking off all my clothes and crawling between the sheets of one of the two neatly turned down beds, but couldn't bear the thought of lying there naked and waiting if he wasn't going to come, and then getting out of bed, putting all my clothes back on and going home. Or worse, falling asleep and waking to a dark and empty room.

I perched myself on the windowsill, the rad below warming me and the cold breeze stinging my face. I searched the windows of the opposite wing of the hotel for another face looking back at me, but there wasn't one. Most of the curtains were closed and there was no telling what was going on behind them: who was being loved, who was watching TV, who was waiting.

Maybe he's dead, I thought. Who'd ever call and tell me, nobody even knew I was here. I could sit in this room for hours, days, weeks while his body grew cold and forgot the memory of mine.

Silly. I was getting silly, and maudlin, and stupid, alone in this room where I couldn't sit still for fear of becoming part of the furniture. I was running out of cigarettes, but was afraid to go out in case he came and thought I'd changed my mind. What if he called? I picked up the telephone receiver to be sure there was a dial tone.

I had to go to the bathroom too, but couldn't because I didn't want him to arrive while I was sitting on the toilet. I didn't want day-to-day details intruding on what should be magic.

I thought of the couple in the airport again. There was nothing out of the ordinary about them. Nothing magic. Except for the pure joy I had found myself standing on the periphery of. They'd get old together, eventually he'd take to calling her Mother, as in: How about another cup of tea, Mother. She'd take to calling him the old fart and complaining when he cut his toenails in bed. And maybe they'd forget that scene in the airport long before I would, but it would always be with them. His arms lifting her higher and higher into the air.

I started to cry all over again, and decided that was it, I would go to the airport and stay there until they could get me a flight home. I was in the bathroom washing my face when I heard the key turn in the lock.

8

I found that I couldn't sleep beside him, and when I turned toward him his body moved away from mine.

I pulled the blanket off the second bed and curled myself into a ball on the armchair, and watched the city lights outside the window. It was getting harder and harder to breathe in the small room even with the window open. I dug through Tom's overnight bag until I found the bottle I knew would be there. I went to the bathroom for a glass, trailing my blanket behind me like the train of a grand wedding-gown.

I poured myself a good shot and raised my glass in a toast to Tom's sleeping form. "It's a helluva long way to come for a lay," I said. His eyelids didn't even flicker. I grabbed the phone book off the desk and dropped it on the floor. Thud. Nothing. So then I picked up the phone and dropped it too. Thud-jangle. And still nothing.

I placed the phone back on the desk and thought about who I could call. I didn't know anybody in this city except an old boyfriend whom I didn't expect would be too happy to hear from me. And then I thought of Tom's wife, sleeping somewhere in the city alone tonight, but I couldn't think of her and breathe at the same time.

I dialled my own number and let it ring once before I hung up. I didn't want to think of Homer in my apartment waiting for me, and even worse was the thought of the apartment empty waiting for my return.

I slipped out of my blanket and climbed up on the windowsill, and pressed my naked body up against the glass, wondering if anybody could see me. When my body was cold and I couldn't hold back the shivers any longer I pulled back the covers and lay my body over Tom's, drawing the warmth from him. When he opened his eyes the first thing I said was: "Talk to me."

"Hello, other world," he said, and I licked his face with my whisky tongue.

When I woke up he was gone. Even though I'd known he was going I'd expected him to stay, to change his mind. To choose me.

9

Homer was waiting for me when I got home.

"I thought you would have gone," I said.

"Thought or hoped?" he asked. He was sitting on the couch, in the dark, naked except for a pair of plaid bedroom slippers that I'd never seen before.

"Don't be silly," I said. "I'm glad you're here. Really."

"I tried to leave, I truly did. I even went home but the other guys had rented out my room and all my plants had died." He pointed to the corner and I saw the skeleton of a fig tree in a huge pot.

"I like it," I said. "It's very minimalist. It makes a statement about—"

"I missed you," he said. "I tried not to, but I did."

"Come talk to me while I unpack," I said. He followed me into the bedroom, walking so close behind me that I could feel his breath on the back of my neck.

"Is it over?" he asked.

"I don't know."

10

Liz phoned first thing the next morning to tell me not to bother coming into work if I was even thinking about it; they canned me when I didn't show up Monday without calling in. I promised to meet her at the bar when she got off work and answer all her questions.

"Homer," I called. He was sleeping on the couch; he'd gotten up in the middle of the night and said sorry, but he couldn't sleep with me when I smelled of someone else.

"Homer," I yelled again. I lit a cigarette and coughed. "I can be anybody now," I said, but there was no answer.

I lay in bed for a long time, my body just a solid mass of weight beneath the covers. I concentrated on removing myself from my body, trying to float a few inches above myself the way they say dying people do. For a moment I made it: I could see myself lying there swaddled in sheets like a newborn. And then I was back. I stayed lying there; it seemed the best thing to do as there was nowhere to go.

Finally I got up because I thought I could smell coffee brewing. Homer wasn't on the couch, or in the kitchen, or anywhere else in the apartment. There wasn't any coffee either.

I was still in bed at six o'clock that night when the security buzzer went. At first I thought it was the alarm clock and it was time to get up for work. It was Liz and she was mad as hell.

When I let her in she said: "Christ, Ruth, you look like shit," and pushed past me into the living-room.

"Where'd you get the twig in a pot?" she asked pointing at Homer's dead fig. "And where the hell have you been? And why didn't you meet me at the goddam bar like you said you would? And who is this Homer guy who's been answering your phone? Is he for real?" She didn't wait for answers, just stormed past me into the kitchen and started banging the cupboard doors.

"Where the hell's the coffee pot?" she yelled at me when I followed her into the kitchen. Bang, bang, crash. "I'm drunk, by the way. I had three lousy Manhattans sitting in the bar by myself, getting eyed by all the leisure suits. Oh here it is." She dumped in some grounds, plugged it in and then sat down gesturing at me to do the same.

"Why'd you do it?" she asked. "Why'd you go back to him?"

"I didn't mean to," I said. "Really I didn't want to. I just did it."

"What's in it for you? Where's the thrill?" Liz got up and unplugged the coffee pot. "I changed my mind," she said and began banging the cupboard doors again.

"Under the sink," I said.

"Ah," she said, pulling out a half-empty bottle of scotch, leftover from the days of Tom. "Serious business here." She poured out two shots, heavy on mine, and then sat down again. "You know," I said. "I've always wanted to love a man to the point of losing all control. To the point of insanity."

Liz just looked at me like I was an imbecile.

I got up and opened a cupboard and pulled out a cast iron skillet. "You see this thing?" I brandished it at her. "My mother gave me this when I got my first apartment; I think she must have gotten it as a wedding present, it's that old. I've never cooked anything in this damn pan, but I'm saving it. You know why?"

Liz just shook her head at me and took a pull off her drink.

"I'm saving it because someday there's going to be a man that I love enough to hate enough and then I'm going to throw the damn thing at him."

Liz just stared at me for a minute and then she started to laugh, rich deep waves of laughter that ended in snorts and gasps for air. I laughed too until the tears came.

II

Tom had given me his number. When am I ever going to use this? I'd asked and he'd laughed but it was a raw sound.

I'd kept the number and one lonely night about a week after Homer did his vanishing act, I found myself dialling it. I had to know if Tom was still there. I told myself if Jacquie answered then I would hang up. It would be like a sign. But when she said hello, her voice thin across the wire, I felt a weird fascination. This was the woman with the red hair, the one that Tom went home to, the one who had it all.

We both listened to the silence and then she said: "I know who you are," real quiet and deadly. "I know all about you." Hang up, I thought, but I couldn't do it. "You really think you're something don't you," she said. "You really think..."

I placed the receiver down on the floor with her voice still spilling out of it and backed out of the room.

I took a bath. I was out of bubble bath so I used the dish soap and it made nice fat bubbles that you could see the world in, upside down. I lay there until the water got too cold, got out, swathed myself in towels and tip-toed into the living-room. The receiver was still lying on the floor and the connection was unbroken. I picked it up and listened.

"Ruth?" Tom's voice. "Is that you, Ruth?"

And then I hung up.

12

Homer came home again. He snuck in while I was asleep and was in bed beside me when I woke.

"I went to the Starlight," he said. "Someone took me home. I wanted to hurt you. I didn't want you to go."

"I know," I said, fitting my body to his.

While he was loving me my eyes were open and I was watching the moon outside the window. Its cruel unblinking eye.

STEVEN HEIGHTON

The Battle of Midway

TOKYO—John Cruikshank, the controversial American journalist, has refused to retract allegations that school textbooks published recently in Japan whitewash the nation's role as an "aggressor" in World War II. He also refused to comment when asked whether American textbooks deliberately ignore the "racial implications" of the U.S. bombing of Hiroshima and Nagasaki. Mr Cruikshank, who is fluent in Japanese, returns to America tomorrow. [from *The Japan Times,* 16 October 1988].

It was our first visit to the house of Mr Fujita Masatomi. It began with a formidably ample meal during which we scandalized our hosts by enjoying raw tuna, then clam, then squid, then (Mrs Fujita having to make a special trip to the kitchen, driven by a sense of baffled desperation and patriotic duty)—several quivering gobbets of raw sea-urchin.

Sensing our hosts' bewilderment and anxiety I diplomatically confessed that while I could stomach the sea-urchin it was not exactly to my taste. I coughed faintly and covered my mouth, as if politely concealing a grimace of disgust.

The day was saved. National pride was salvaged and restored. My wife deftly consolidated this little victory by preferring coffee when offered either that or Japanese tea.

The time had come, our host solemnly decreed, for interesting conversation. I fell back on a trusty gambit. I told him, in Japanese, that I found his house very comfortable and his *tokonoma* particularly impressive. Mr Fujita turned to his brother and wife and the rest of his large family and told them, in Japanese, that I found the house very comfortable and the *tokonoma* particularly impressive. In clear English his daughter told us I was being unnecessarily polite: it was an old house and nothing to get excited about. Mr Fujita and his family, who did not understand English, grinned and nodded as if to corroborate this remark, which I therefore took as a standard expression of modesty. No, I insisted in fornal Japanese, you are quite wrong, your house is actually very nice.

My words seemed to come as a bit of a surprise to Mr Fujita but he turned and repeated them to his family as before. His daughter maintained that the house was unremarkable, was in fact rather ugly, and noted there were problems with the plumbing. In Japanese I told her the plumbing had seemed fine on my last visit to the washroom, which, in conventional Japanese manner, I compared favourably with our own humble facilities. Mr Fujita shot a quick glance at his daughter. She said in English that she hated living at home and would certainly leave if she were a few years older. In Japanese I told Mr Fujita he had a charming girl. Not at all, he said, resorting to the traditional phrase, not at all…

It had been a heavy lunch. We were all getting tired. My wife's face had that ominously inflated look that shows she's smothering a yawn; Mr Fujita's brother leaned back from the low table as if to stretch himself full-length on the *tatami* and did not stir for the rest of the afternoon.

"The old folks are always sleeping," Mr Fujita's daughter complained. "Sometimes it's impossible to wake them up."

Mr Fujita barked a command in brusque Japanese. His children wheeled a television set and a VCR into the room while he selected a tape and loaded the machine. Everyone (except Mr Fujita's sleeping brother) moved briskly to their new stations. Cups and scraps of food were efficiently evacuated. I had the feeling that if the premises were searched, a detailed schedule of the afternoon's proceedings would sooner or later appear.

Karaoke, Mr Fujita announced, beaming in anticipation. He drew a large microphone from a drawer under the VCR and plugged it into the speaker of the TV set. For some time I had been expecting this to happen.

Mr Fujita performed scales to warm up.

"*Karaoke* means 'empty orchestra,'" Mr Fujita's daughter explained. I told her in Japanese that I knew it. "Empty," she went on in English, "because there is only music and no voice." She swept her hand in a full circle to take in all present, then pointed at the microphone.

"We make the words ourselves," she said.

"You mean we read them," I corrected her, nodding toward the television where a glowing white pellet, like a grain of cooked rice, romped from character to character as a lyric crossed the screen....

A western model rode a black stallion along the edge of the Inland Sea as Mr Fujita crooned a traditional lament in his excellent baritone. Mr Fujita's daughter sang "My way"—a Western song that almost every Japanese knows. My wife and I were urged to sing a duet. A quick survey of programs showed that only one other English song, "Yesterday," was available to us, and finally Mr Fujita found it on an old disused cassette. He hoped the quality was still reasonable.

It was. The video featured a brylcreemed teenager brooding among cherry trees over a wallet-full of tiny photographs. The woman in the photographs was visibly blond.

We bungled the song badly before returning the microphone.

Suddenly the footage accompanying the lyrics switched from garish colour into the shuddering, scratchy black-and-white of vintage newsreels. Small airplanes swooped in formation toward a burning aircraft carrier, big guns fired from the armoured decks of battleships. Two Zero fighters could be seen crashing into the sea. Mr Fujita's cozy den was filled with the sounds of battle.

I nudged my wife. "Pearl Harbour?" she whispered, her lips contorted like a ventriloquist's. I told her it looked like

Midway. I wondered if our hosts were hinting that it was time to leave.

Mr Fujita's face was now the blanched tint of the raw cuttle-fish we had eaten an hour before. His kneeling body was perfectly rigid yet seemed somehow to be inching toward the television set, like a machine on hidden ball bearings. Music had started up, the voiceless score of an old Beatles' tune, and Japanese lyrics crossed the screen in silver spurts like the glimmering tracks of tracer bullets.

"I think it's 'All You Need Is Love,'" my wife whispered, beginning to giggle. I pinched her foot. "Don't you dare," I hissed.

Some of the children watched the screen while others played around Mr Fujita's peaceful brother, who lay like a casualty on the deck of a destroyer. His daughter watched the battle with rapt attention, as if she had never seen anything like it before.

Mr Fujita had now manoeuvred his mysterious body to within striking distance of the VCR. He grinned immensely as his hand shot out at the on-off switch beside the screen. He missed. The volume rose exponentially and the den thundered with explosions and the sound of tubas and trombones straining toward a crescendo. The fallen brother twitched in his sleep, as if having a bad dream. Mr Fujita's fingers found the on-off switch and the television went dark, just as a Zero fighter on a *kamikaze* mission whizzed into the deck of an aircraft carrier.

"*Ma, jubun desu,*" Mr Fujita said. "That's enough television for now. The children tend to watch too much, you know. The daughter especially."

The daughter frowned. "He's full of it," she said in English.

Mrs Fujita burst from the kitchen with a fresh pot of coffee. The daughter began to whisper in my wife's ear; my wife struggled to contain a smile. The children were running around the room with their arms extended, making engine noises, pretending to be airplanes. The brother trembled again in his sleep.

Sounds of the Water

The old pond, ah!
A frog jumps in—
the water's sound
—Basho.

Jason holds the shower nozzle above his head and feels icy water course through his hair and over his face. His eyes are tightly closed. In his nostrils and around his parted lips the water forms clots and running pools, like a stream cascading over gaps and fissures in a tropical cliff. Jason breathes steadily, enjoying the illusion that he can survive in two elements.

He is a frog, or some scaly, exotic amphibian—the member of a scarce and endangered species. A cliff-toad peering from a ledge through the veil of a waterfall, vigilant for predators. An injured bullfrog, blinking hungrily, bathing its wounds in the dim pool of a Kyoto garden. The old pond, ah!

Jason's mother has begun to call him. He can barely hear her through the locked door and over the sounds of the water. Her voice reaches him in baritone spasms—much like the voice of his father, or like ripples of thunder during the monsoon. A light quick tinkling is the ping of raindrops on stepping stones outside a Chinese teahouse (or the emergency key twisting in the bathroom lock).

As the door bursts open he leans back into the tub and submerges. His wide-open frog's eyes stare up through the water at a dim unfocused form which raises wobbling arms to its head and emits a muffled scream.

It is Christmas and I am a child of ten. My sister and I sit by the drooping tree among empty boxes and tangled scraps of tinsel and dappled paper. In the curls above my sister's ear, like some rare Pacific flower, I have set a magenta bow. As the lights on

the tree flicker the bow glitters in her hair and her calm face is
suffused with a marvellous light. I reach out to her with
another bow. In my lap is the marble-green globe I have just
pulled from a cardboard box.

Father was a full-time world traveller of part-time renown, a
renegade, a rogue male, a foreign correspondent who did not
correspond, an absence and a distance, a jumbo-jet gypsy with
a rakish leer and leather briefcase full of farewell cards and
polyester flowers. Our house was too small for him. Likewise
our town and our family. He was a lady-killer—no mean
suburban beau but a gallant cavalier whose ambitions were
truly global. In the winter he wore a great fur coat and clapped
his hands and breathed long streams of mist into the freezing
air as he talked of Mongolia. He used words we could not
understand and did not notice or did not care that their meaning was lost on us. He was alien and exotic. When we met him
at the airport his arms were always bursting with strange gifts
and he carried in his clothes and on his breath faint odours
that were new to us. He was The Craw, the great furry ursine
beast that pursued us through the dark basement and up half-
lit flights of stairs and even into our dreams as we squealed in
an ecstasy of fear. He was venerable and distant, a compelling
will roaming the house between assignments, a brooding
absence when he was away.

Beside him Mother was staid and pious, gentle, competent
and methodical, perpetually consoling. All the photographs
we have of her are slightly blurred. Someone seems to have
tampered with my memories of her, for her face always has a
soft focus, as if in deference to an actress prematurely aged. We
can see now that her compliance and reserve dissembled a
mounting despair, and we can feel, as of course we could not
feel then, admiration for her stamina. My father knew what
he was doing when he married her. Perhaps he was as sur-

prised as we were the one time she fell from character (the actress, prematurely aged) and became a foreigner to us, as he had always been.

In those days I was always in retreat, always searching for undiscovered corners. In anonymous nooks and clefts and attics, pantries, cupboards and crawl-spaces, in steamer trunks or hidden in the laundry hamper under father's well-travelled clothing, I would stow away for hours.

I was never hungry; I did not get bored. A menagerie of illusions sustained me and like an emperor's magician I could assume the outward form of any creature in the Animal Kingdom. That morning, like a cub or a tree frog, I had wedged myself under our crooked pine and was gazing up into the living-room through a dense screen of twigs and needles. Bulbs winked a few inches from my eyes, ornaments dangled. No-one knew I was there. Through all the foliage, coloured lights and cramped glass spheres, I could not see the expressions on my parents' faces, though of course I could distinguish their words and the tones that gave them meaning.

My mother, cautiously: "David, you know it wasn't what he wanted."

"Sometimes it's best to get things you think you don't want."

"David. David, look, you know why you gave him the book. We both know why. Because it's what you would have wanted at his age. What you'd still want." Surprisingly firm. Gathering momentum and with it confidence. Becoming strident.

"Well? How else can I decide what to give him?" Alerted, surprised.

"You don't know who he is. You don't care. You think he's just a shadow—your shadow. You want him to be your shadow. You want him to grow up to be like you, to think like you—" With a kind of disbelief, as if the airing of the words has crystallized a terrifying, latent recognition.

"And you don't."

"Why should I? You think I want to be abused by my own son?"

"Who's abused? I bought him a nice book. He loves it."

"It's you who loves the book, David. You don't know the first thing about how he feels. You don't know how any of us feel you're so wrapped up in yourself. You never listen when the children tell you things or ask you questions and you never listen to me."

"You never speak."

"I make a point of speaking to you whenever you drop in. But nothing gets through to you, does it? When you're happy the whole world should sing with you and if it won't you blame us all for upsetting the harmony. When you're mad because an assignment's not going well or you're blocked then everyone else had better sympathize or else they're insensitive and cruel and—"

"Marilyn, for God's sake, it's Christmas."

"You make me feel like it's my fault."

"Are you so sure it's all mine?"

"You expect me to take the blame for everything. Fifteen years. You act as if she's my fault too. I'm letting myself go, I don't watch what I eat, I'm always asleep by the time you get to bed—and then you hint at how much better things would have been for you if you hadn't married me—"

"This isn't like you, Marilyn."

"You don't know what I'm like. You don't care."

"Marilyn, for Christ's sake…"

I coughed then—as an animal caught out of its element might struggle for breath. I coughed again, louder. I knew my father would do angry things soon after he used those words. *For Christ's sake.* I knew the pale, featureless orbs turning abruptly in my direction were the faces of my parents. Their sudden silence was more terrifying than their voices had been.

"Jason," my mother's voice said, "Jason, we didn't know you—"

"What do you mean by hiding under there while we're talking, Jason? Come out from under there. Now."

"Jason, darling, Daddy and I"

"Out of there. Come on."

"weren't aware that"

"Now."

I saw my father's body squatting and waddling toward the tree. His movements were awkward. He did not belong down here. His face was still obscured by the cool-smelling boughs, the rich odour of pine like the scent around ponds in Kyoto. I picked up the book he had given me, *A Journey Through Asia*, and retreated toward the farthest edge of the tree. An enormous hand reached under the rustling boughs and groped directly toward me. Shaken ornaments swayed and rattled. One fell and shattered on the floor. Leave him alone, my mother cried, leave the boy alone.

"The Craw," my father called. "The Craw wants his Christmas dinner!"

"No," I yelled feebly. "Go away."

I felt the hand on my wrist. I willed it away. I saw my father's vast white face follow his arm into the open under the boughs, like a moon setting in a jungle clearing. "The Craw wants his turkey," the face cried. "But I'm a frog!" I screamed. And shut my eyes so I would not have to see.

It was no ordinary globe my father bequeathed me. Though I lost it years ago I can still remember every facet and feature of it. Where the land met the cobalt sea it was green as our neighbours' lawns and if you moved your finger along the coastlines you felt the shore rising out of the water. The land continued to rise—you could feel it with your finger—and turned a sun-burnt brown then yellow then chilly white for the snow-covered peaks. The poles were a frosty, monotonous silver. When I slid my fingers over Antarctica I could feel the rise and fall of massifs under the ice-sheet, and imagined I could feel the biting cold of the glaciers. The deserts were a dusty yellow, the coast of Siberia an ominous white. The scattered volcanic islands of Japan reared suddenly from the sea's trenches. And most of all I remember the high plateau of Tibet, its egg-shaped swelling crowned with a craggy shell of silver; how I loved to travel my fingers along its roughness and, as if it con-tained a code, a passage in braille, abstracted images of the day I would stand there, hours above the rest of the world, over the steaming succulent jungles of Thailand and the vast grain-fields of China (my fingertips, journeying), over the war-torn countries where my father often went, over Burma, over Nepal, the boreal forests of Siberia, the Indonesian archi-pelagoes, the seething metropolises of India and the outskirts of Brampton, Ontario.

In the days between Christmas and New Year's, the globe and the book *A Journey Through Asia* were always in my hands. In favour of these gifts all stuffed animals, save two, were ousted from my bed. Only Agnew the patched, tattered lamb and Basho, the stuffed frog my father had just brought back from Japan, escaped closet exile.

When he came home my father brought gifts for my mother, too, but for some reason they always made her cry.

On New Year's Eve, Pandora and I were playing the globe-game in her room. One of us had to wear a blindfold while the other held out the globe; the blindfolded player would reach out and feel the proffered surface and on that flimsy basis name the part touched. My sister was deplorably bad at this game. I was always giving her clues. "Dad went there last Easter," I'd say. *He's always going places.* "Last Tuesday," I'd venture, "do you remember what Mom made for dinner last Tuesday?" *Nope.* "Curry! She made curry!" *So?* "A kind of ink," I'd hiss, "beginning with 'I.' Elephants. Sitars. Silk." *I give up.* "So do I," I'd groan, giving the globe a half turn.

"Now," I said to her, "try again."

"Ummmm…"

"Come on, it's easy."

"Maybe with a little hint…"

"Pearl Harbour," I whispered tentatively. "Chopsticks."

"It feels like a little mouseturd under my finger."

"You idiot. Do you know what the samurai would do to you for saying that?"

"I give up. Let's play another game."

"Ah so! Honourable sister-san not want to continue!"

"Germany! It's Germany! Mrs Schmidt always says 'Ah so' in gym class."

"You're hopeless," I cried, braining her with the cardboard globe to make her stop laughing. But she would not stop. And I wanted to hit her again. The more ridiculous her mistakes were, the more she giggled. It frustrated me that my triumphs failed to chasten her or make her more serious—it wasn't at all like winning a game against boys. But at least she was impressed by my talents. I knew the globe so well that I could guess the correct location almost every try. I told her I could even distinguish the icy chill of the North Atlantic from the placid warmth of the South Pacific—and though I used coastlines to help me discriminate, I almost believed my boast was true.

Finally she stumped me on Southern Ontario. "Brampton!" she cheered. "It's our own place! Don't you know?"

I didn't. But this little lapse didn't affect her admiration for me; she insisted we show Mom and Dad what I could do. "Daddy can write an article about you for the travel magazines," she said earnestly. "Now he won't have to go away to find his stories."

We walked together up the dim hall to my parents' room. I cradled the globe under my arm like a helmet. Their door was closed, they would be readying themselves for the neighbours' New Year's Eve party.

I heard voices from beyond the door but they were not my parents'. I couldn't make out the words. I heard a sharp sound. I tried to say something to my sister but in her excitement she had already turned the doorknob and was pushing open the door. "Daddy! Mommy! See what Jason can do!"

At odd times ever since I have seen them again as they were, momentarily frozen as in a Christmas tableau. I have a good memory. The scene does not change. Framed within the doorway they are two exotic natives surprised in the front room of their hut by an intrepid photographer. Familiar features of the room and of their persons have taken on a primitive and alien aspect, an air of inscrutable treachery: Father standing in profile, his back to the mirror, facing my mother who is facing us. Her eyes meeting ours but not acknowledging this accident. Their bodies tensed, faces still. Suddenly a small dark bead like a jewel forming at the corner of my mother's mouth and trickling rapidly down her chin.

My father's eyes turn toward us slowly, inexorably as in a dream, his thin lips snarling, the doorbell, can't either of you hear the doorbell? Go and let the babysitter in.

At breakfast the next morning his parents are hungover and in no mood for his games.

"Take off the blindfold, Jason," his father says.

"Do what your father tells you," says his mother.

His sister giggles hysterically for a moment then begins to cry.

Jason explains that the blindfold is part of the globegame,

which he offers to demonstrate after breakfast, but Father says he has to call the travel agent after breakfast and Mother says she doesn't feel well and will lie down. Jason has never heard his mother say anything like this before. He is having breakfast with two strangers who may or may not turn out to be friendly.

Dora asks their mother if it's her mouth that's bothering her because she has a cut there doesn't she and Jason is glad he is wearing the blindfold so he does not have to see the cut or watch his mother's face as the question hits home.

"Your blindfold, Jason," his father rumbles. "Take it off."

"That's not in the rules," Jason says with pressed dignity, stumbling from the table and feeling his way toward the stairs.

The blindfold curtails Jason's studies but he has read enough of *A Journey Through Asia* that he can imagine and extrapolate and surmise. He turns the globe slowly in his hands and hears through the wall of the study his father's voice arranging and reserving flights for an excursion to Tibet. Usually he hears little through the wall but in the short time since he began wearing the blindfold his hearing has become preternaturally acute, like the faculties of some nocturnal creature.

First his father is talking softly, there is a sense of urgency in his voice, urgency and explanation. Now another call, a different tone. Clearer. There will be fighting in Tibet very soon, he hears, and if you get me in now before they close the borders I'll be there when it happens. Yes. Yes. I may have to stay awhile. A photographer too. Fine. One of the new hotels. Lhasa via Hong Kong and Chengdu? Yes. Fine. Jason moves his fingers over the Himalayan plateau and its oval swelling feels to him like an incipient tumour or permanent scar. Fighting there. But who? In *A Journey Through Asia* Tibet was a peaceful kingdom (his father's voice stops and a door slams outside as he leaves the study)—a peaceful kingdom high up

above the rest of the world: the ravenous tiger-eyed jungles of
Burma, the bloody banks of the river Jordan, barren tundra
along the frozen seas, the starving cities of Bangladesh and the
outskirts of Brampton, Ontario. In Tibet all the people had
serene meditative expressions because the air was too thin for
fighting. If you tried to argue you would hyperventilate and if
you actually swung your fist at someone you would have a
heart attack and die. Jason had not read these exact things but
his inferences were solidly founded. In Tibet the thin air made
people giddy and they laughed at everything you said. There
were no comedians in Tibet because the idea of needing to
make people laugh was alien to the Tibetans. The Tibetans
never dreamed. There was no need to escape through dream-
ing, or by any other means, like some amphibian forced to
exchange elements in order to survive. In Tibet everyone
inhabited the same element: in the crisp vivid air of the high
plain things appeared as they really were, and the light was too
brilliant and clear for lying. Lamas walked through the
temples, gentle furry mammals in orange robes, the sacred
cows of Tibet. Having animals as spiritual and political leaders
must have many advantages....

Jason's father is in the study again, speaking rapidly and
quietly on the phone. Even with his superior hearing Jason
can make out only a few words. *No...overseas soon...
anymore...court? Marilyn* (his mother's name)...*Marilyn.* And
the word *childsupport.* He has never heard this word before. It
makes him think immediately of his mother. *Marilyn. Yes. Yes.
Goodbye.* His father's door slams again. He hears him calling
his mother to come upstairs. Putting the globe down, Jason
slips quietly through his door and into the bathroom. He
locks the door and climbs into the tub. For the first time in
several days he removes his blindfold—and has to close his
eyes immediately because of the unaccustomed light. As his
parents begin to converse somewhere in the distance he holds

the shower nozzle like a phone receiver above his head and feels icy water course through his hair and over his face. His eyes are tightly closed.

At dinner Jason is scolded—no doubt for locking the bathroom door and terrifying his mother. This is his deduction, based on the infrequent words that penetrate his silent world. He has stuffed both ears with wads of cotton. He has refused to remove his blindfold and will say nothing but the word "No."

"To hell with it," he makes out distinctly. "Let the kid do...he wants. Your...son."

But at bedtime first his father then his mother come into his room. Though their words are filtered out by the cotton plugs, the tone and tenor of their voices are unmistakable. They are solicitous, sympathetic. He hears his father: Jason...Doctor? He shakes his head to signal No. The word itself now seems an extravagant concession.

Eyes...hurting?

Go away, he commands him in his mind, reckoning slyly that his father's obedience is sooner or later assured. In fact he gathers his father is leaving in a few days. And now some kind of promise is being made—probably of gifts from Tibet.

Suddenly Jason speaks. Will his father see the Dalai Lama? No...exile...India. Look, take that...stuff out of...ears.

Exile! Jason cries. How could they ever send him out of his own country? Why would they want to do it?

Politics, he hears faintly, *politics,* as if the word is being shouted over a vast distance.

Why...blindfold?

But he's just an animal, Jason cries, he's innocent!

His father says something he doesn't catch, but in the dull, distant rumble of the voice, like a whirlpool nearing on a wide river, he hears a wistful, inexorable sadness so unlike his father he wants to tear off his blindfold and see who is there. But he is afraid. He senses the huge, whiskery face lingering above his own, and wonders if the doubt and indecision he feels is his own or his father's. The two faces hover in the darkness together, like a planet and a moon. Jason pictures a pool in a lush jungle brimming with moonlight, in the breathless moment before the predator springs, and senses there is still something he might say. But he does not know what it is.

Jason does not tear off his blindfold. After a gentle, hurried kiss his father's face breaks away from him and recedes into the darkness.

When his mother comes in she says nothing—or perhaps she is only whispering. He senses her beside him, inhabiting the silences, warming and disarming them. When she kisses him goodnight he feels the moisture on her cheeks and around her lips.

Jason plays the globegame with Dora or sits alone in his room. For her he will remove his cotton plugs. She is sad because she never sees Mommy and Daddy. They are always in their room talking or going out somewhere in the car again and again. They go out suddenly and though they are never long they leave no babysitter and Dora is afraid. Mommy isn't being Mommy anymore. There's never any dinner. And Jason— aren't you getting hungry? How long is it since you've ate?

She wonders if they'll both go away to China this time. He tells her no.

One day in his father's study he removes his blindfold and finds a pair of genuine earplugs. The picture on the tiny packet shows a passenger in an airplane sleeping peacefully while two strangers rant and gesticulate beside him. With some difficulty Jason extracts two sticky wads of cotton from his ears and inserts the traveller's earplugs. Only the loudest of sounds, the packet guarantees, can violate them.

Probably it is only a day or two, but it seems as if many months go by while Jason hibernates in his soundless world. His mind roams without agenda over an uneven past and through the Asia of his Christmas reading—and finds Asia by far the more hospitable locale. As he stumbles unintentionally onto the scene where his father refuses absolutely to allow pets in the house, No, not even the Shepherd puppy that has trailed Dora home from the park, he struggles to escape and finds himself in the bow of a golden schooner in some Asian sea. But in Asia there are disturbing visions, too. More vivid than many things he has actually witnessed he sees the photograph in his book showing a statue of the fasting Buddha. Sharp, appalling bones protrude through the figure's skin like the ribs of the crucified Christ his mother retrieves from the basement each Christmas. The statue sits by a pond in a Kyoto garden. Behind it, silhouetted against the water, is the bough of a plum tree heavy with fruit. What is it that makes the stone figure so reluctant to eat? Why are the sunken eyes closed so resolutely on that tranquil scene? A caption reminds readers that at last the Buddha renounced his austerity and chose the path of moderation, but clearly there had been a time when he was unable to accept and assimilate anything his surroundings offered. Jason thinks of Lamas sauntering up the halls of their hermitage toward the refectory, their blunt velvety snouts sniffing air perfumed with the scents of tea and *tsampa*. But some of them were in exile. They would be isolated and hungry.

His belly growls, and like a lion-tamer he quells it with a brisk slap. He has eaten nothing. This has not been like a real Christmas at all, except for the book and the globe, and the magenta bow in his sister's curls, and the way the coloured lights flashed and glittered over her face. Last Christmas was not real either, or the one before that, but Mother was more in control then and the troubles were quieter, present but contained, like something packed skillfully in a delicate box. He remembers unwrapping *A Journey Through Asia* on Christmas Eve and thinks of those Asian kings in the passage his mother always asks father to read them then: *now when Jesus was born in Bethlehem of Judea in the days of Herod the king, behold, wise men from the East came unto Jerusalem....*

Where had the wise men come from? And how? His father couldn't tell him. One was from Japan, he thinks to himself, and wore armour studded with jewels and brought with him a jade statue of the enlightened Buddha. Another from India rode a tattooed elephant and carried silks and nutmeg, twigs of cinnamon, mangoes and diamonds the size of pelicans' eggs. The third was the Dalai Lama himself, ambling on his gentle hoofs, bearing on his saffron-robed spine exotic testaments and maps and scriptures. And they were wise. That was a rare thing. Something that would dwell, furtive and endangered, in the very heart of Asia. Perhaps his father was looking for it on his travels. Someday Jason must go.

On the last day of the Christmas holidays he and his mother and sister accompany his father to the airport; like a seeing-eye dog, his sister leads him through the terminal's automatic doors. Even through his earplugs Jason can hear the crowds, and he is dazzled by countless fluorescent lights when he finally takes off his blindfold because his mother has knelt beside him and removed one earplug and begged him please to be sensible, his father is leaving for a long time, won't he be a good boy and say goodbye?

At the time he attaches no significance to his father's visit to the counter of a domestic airline before checking in for his international flight, but he knew even then with the deaf-and-dumb intuition of a child that his father would not be coming back, ever. His mother is crying discreetly and his sister giggling the way she still does now when she's nervous or afraid of betraying some inappropriate emotion. His father refusing to look directly at any of them. His face like an ancient statue's, perfected in its stolid grief, as if resolved not to fracture into pitiful decay despite its antiquity. He sees it that way now. He remembers nothing of his actual feelings as he and Dora struggle to lift an unprecedented second suitcase onto the scale, and his father disappears into customs after hurried kisses and a vague guarantee of gifts on his return.

Years after making his own journey to Asia, these scenes he thought he'd escaped return to him. He is in his apartment, alone, watching a National Geographic special on the Bering Straits. From Alaska the camera pans across a dark expanse of water hemmed in by fog, while an authoritative voice explains that in clear weather one can see hills on the coast of Asia. Abrupt cut to a view of the same water under sunny skies and there they are, as promised, pale hills rising over the Siberian coast, hills the voice describes as the remnants of the Great Bering Land Bridge. *"By which men once crossed from Asia to North America,"* the voice goes on, becoming animated as it explains that since the bridge disappeared the only animal able to cross the straits is the polar bear. *"What amazes the crews of isolated Bering Sea oilrigs are the bears that will sometimes appear in the surrounding water, as much as 60 miles from Siberia, the nearest land, and 100 miles from the Alaskan coast where the bears must have originated..."* As the scene cuts to the deck of an oil-rig, Jason sees men in dirty parkas lining the rails and cheering at a small unfocused spot of white bobbing in the rough grey seas. The camera zooms unsteadily and a white bear is seen to turn its head for a moment as if to acknowledge the crew's attention, then continue aloofly on its way.

Wandering back through the enormous airport, struggling with holiday crowds, we pass counters studded with long queues and giftshops full of books and postcards on rotating stands. Our mother is perfectly composed. She is herself again, patient and predictable, vulnerable, necessary. Smiling her kind, conspiratorial smile she reaches down and pulls the remaining plug from my ear. Dora has stopped giggling and is pointing with wonder at a huge globe revolving above a ticket counter. Our mother nods and smiles. As we pass a restaurant she suggests we get a meal.

A Protruding Nail

deru kugi wa utareru

Midway through a learned sermon on the origin and implications of various Japanese proverbs, Mr. Sato Takaharu urbanely interrupted himself. His voice bristled with irony as he asked a small girl for her favourite *kotowaza*.

The girl was Kaizaki Sachiko and she was completely at a loss—exactly as *sensei* had anticipated. He had noticed some time before that she was paying no attention to his lecture and was not taking any notes. She was what the staff of the school, in their wittier moments, liked to refer to as a "gazer."

—Sachiko, the looming Mr Sato reverberated. Sachiko, from the beginning of this class, and, indeed, the beginning of term—(a pause for the ensuing round of delighted laughter)—you have obstinately refused to attend to your studies, both in class and at home. Moving you away from the windows seems not to have had the remedial effect I intended. You continue to gaze toward the windows. You are in fact a gazer (another pause, more laughter)—and idle gazing is one form of negligence I find absolutely intolerable. I shall ask again: what is your favourite *kotowaza*?

Silence for a moment. Sachiko's intoxicated classmates prayed she would say nothing so that the titillating harangue might continue. Everyone knew Mr Sato was the hardest teacher in the school, and he himself sensed (with a stab of pleasure) that students preferred his spectacular ambushes to the study of familiar proverbs. These students were far too young for his scholarship. He flushed with shame and anger as he recalled the university, his demotion...

—Come, Sachiko, he crooned to immediate acclaim (the laughter choking her, drawing tears to her eyes)—We know you're a clever child!

And in fact she did know her proverbs, even if she neglected to take notes. A clever child, as he had said. It came to her in a fit of inspiration:

—With flattery even a pig can be made to climb a tree.

Mr. Sato reddened as the class loosed a typhoon of laughter. Flattery, after all, was the device of servants and merchants, corporate flunkies and career politicians. The ingenuity of Sachiko's choice was obvious even to her classmates. And it was their attentive presence that seemed to infuriate *sensei* most; children could be drilled till they learned to retain as many facts as a small computer, but no child needed drilling to remember amusing insults, successful pranks, humiliating confrontations. They were unsurpassable when it came to that. This incident was already stored in their memories. It would cling to his reputation, an unsightly protrusion, like a wad of chewing-gum stuck to the blackboard.

Mr. Sato staggered away from Sachiko's desk and spun in a full circle, screaming for quiet.

Such laughter was completely unsuitable.

This instance of irresponsible hilarity constituted a serious breach of classroom etiquette. Harsh and immediate disciplinary measures were indicated. And Sachiko, on whose (narrow, delicate) shoulders full responsibility for all punitive action ultimately rested, was to leave the room and not return until Mr. Sato had duly considered the situation and conferred with her parents, whom he intended to notify at once. Go!

Sachiko obeyed with difficulty, stumbling between desks, impeded by cunningly extended legs and the tears that filled and clouded her eyes. She found herself outside the classroom in the sunlit corridor and heard the door slam closed behind her with the sound Mr. Sato's metre-stick made when he slashed it onto the desks of gazers.

The sunlight through the clean glass wall of the corridor

blinded her. She paused to wipe tears from her eyes. Behind her she could hear Mr. Sato continuing his lecture with a terrifying new zeal:

—And of course the adage you will be most familiar with and which indeed is well known even overseas is one about whose provenance there is still some debate, though Murata insists it must have arisen first in the Edo region and adduces as evidence several cogent items we will later discuss. It is fascinating in this connection that the foreign scholars Fletcher and Stromsky argue that almost every language has evolved a maxim of similar import though nowhere perhaps does it enjoy such currency as in our country with the possible exception of several obscure societies that we will later discuss. Will anyone in the class recite this slogan for our collective benefit? You, Mr Inoue, ought to know it. Eh? What was that? Would you do us the favour of repeating yourself audibly?

THE NAIL THAT STICKS UP GETS HAMMERED DOWN.

—Thank you. Allow me to repeat that.

Sachiko shuffles up the sunlit corridor with the suave modulations of Mr. Sato and the cowed, hysterical tone of Inoue Haruo's voice following her toward the far door. THE NAIL THAT STICKS UP. Makes her think of the mistaken nail-head in the frame of the window she used to sit beside. It sticks up a little. She used to stare at it. Gaze. She took a curious pride and comfort in its lopsided imperfection. *Sensei* hadn't noticed it yet and she was worried that her staring at the window might draw his attention to the little flaw. He would call in his superiors, who would inspect the deviant frame with a mounting sense of outrage and disgrace. The Inspector of Schools would be notified and a committee appointed to investigate and rectify the error. The Minister of Education would visit the school and apologize in person to an assembly of parents and, should he feel the situation were of sufficient gravity, tender his resignation. Letters would be written In that tone of diplomatic hostility reserved elsewhere for declarations of war. Across the country woodworkers' unions would protest their competence. But heads would roll. GETS HAMMERED DOWN.

And all this time, Sachiko muses, pushing open the door and stepping out into the dirty spring air, he thinks I was looking out the window. Stood by my desk and looked in the same direction to see what I was always gazing at. Factories, streets, garages, smokestacks, cram-schools. It was that nail. He'll find it now. He will. He can't miss it. A crooked little bulge speckled with white paint like the egg of that arctic bird we learned about in class. I pretended the warm sun through the windows would hatch it. It was like an ancient sundial—as the lessons passed, tiny shadows moved around it and I always knew the time. In winter during the tutorials after school the shadows covered it and it was pale grey like the plum blossoms in Nagai Park that get rained on all March. Sometimes a little snow falls too and when it melts the blossoms are bleached white like the tips of your fingers on a cold morning in February as you walk to school, or on Saturdays to the cram-school across the tracks from the park, with the plum blossoms beginning and a little wet snow still falling between the trees....

Sachiko shuffling across a corner of Nagai Park on her way home, worried about the fate of an unconforming nail. She knows south Osaka has not received more than a dusting of snow in a hundred years. She has learned it in class.

...and the snow falling and falling the world white and traffic disappearing the railway tracks covered with drifts between trains snow thickening on the roofs in tall plumes blocking the tips of chimneys of factories the high windows of pachinko houses and schools until Nagai Park is white as Hokkaido

then with my lunch pail through growing drifts of shredded paper, cheeks glowing with cold like the seals like arctic hares running north to the frozen shore I learned once there were packs of wolves there and white bears swim in the sea